More praise for

FIERCER MONSTERS

Whether he is recasting the Tower of Babel story with forest creatures saved by a shamanic chihuahua, or deciphering Arabish text slang in the mind of a tortured prisoner whose last refuge—that of his imagination— is threatening to implode, Youssef Alaoui is never merely out to entertain, though the richness of his metaphors and the kookiness of his tales do not fail to charm and delight. No, Alaoui is engaged in a fiercer struggle, between cultures intent on destroying each other and themselves, in the cavernous gaps between what can be felt and known and what can be spoken and understood. Vibrantly lonely, steeped in the sad funk of human pathos, the fables and incantations in *Fiercer Monsters* sing from the belly, from the groin, from the broken bone, and from the whole and sheltering heart.

— **SARAH FRAN WISBY, author of** *The Heart's Progress* **(2014)**

FIERCER MONSTERS

YOUSSEF ALAOUI

NOMADIC PRESS

OAKLAND
2926 FOOTHILL BOULEVARD #1
OAKLAND, CA 94601

2301 TELEGRAPH AVENUE
OAKLAND, CA 94612

BROOKLYN
475 KENT AVENUE #302
BROOKLYN, NY 11249

WWW.NOMADICPRESS.ORG

MASTHEAD
FOUNDING AND EXECUTIVE DIRECTOR
J. K. FOWLER

ASSOCIATE EDITOR
MICHAELA MULLIN

DESIGN
BRITTA FITHIAN-ZURN

MISSION STATEMENT
Nomadic Press is a 501 (C)(3) not-for-profit organization
that supports the works of emerging and established
writers and artists. Through publications (including
translations) and performances, Nomadic Press aims
to build community among artists and across disciplines.

SUBMISSIONS
Nomadic Press wholeheartedly accepts unsolicited
book manuscripts, as well as pieces for our annual
Nomadic Journal. To submit your work, please visit:
www.nomadicpress.org/submissions

DISTRIBUTION
Orders by trade bookstores and wholesalers:
please contact Small Press Distribution,
1341 Seventh Street, Berkeley, CA 94701
spd@spdbooks.org
(510) 524-1668 / (800) 869-7553 (Toll Free)

© 2017 by Youssef Alaoui

This book was made possible by a loving community of family and friends, old and new.

For author questions or to book a reading at your bookstore, university/school,
or alternative establishment, please send an email to info@nomadicpress.org.

Cover Art by Lena Rushing (lenarushing.com)

Published by Nomadic Press, 2926 Foothill Boulevard, Oakland, California, 94601

First printing, 2017

Printed in the United States of America

Library of Congress Cataloging-in-Publication Data

Fiercer Monsters
p. cm.
Summary: Youssef Alaoui's short-story collection, *Fiercer Monsters*, is concerned with the
symbology of letters and the word as invocation, contrasted with the futility of language.
In these stories, Alaoui presents a Neanderthal oracle, a little girl in Venezuela in the 1950s,
a 19th-century hallucinating sailor, and a WWI soldier. The voices are sometimes salty, always
salient. Each voice ultimately laments the fall of the tower of Babel and the resulting confusion.

[1. Fiction/Short Stories. 2. History/Middle East/General.] I. III. Title.

2017902346

ISBN: 978-0-9981348-2-6

FIERCER MONSTERS

YOUSSEF ALAOUI

NOMADIC
PRESS

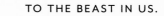

TO THE BEAST IN US.

We have already gone beyond whatever we have words for.
In all talk there is a grain of contempt.

— FRIEDRICH NIETZSCHE
Twilight of the Idols

Contents

FOREWORD

Somewhere in this world of ours at this very moment, there is a writer holding their head in their hands and wondering "Why do I do this? Why do any of us do this?"

It's a question that comes up with the literati at their social gatherings. Inevitably another writer (often a poet working on full carafe #2) will invoke a devotion to the craft of The Word as if words could be imbued with the sacred characteristics of a grail. I'll be honest: for me, I don't buy it. But that's not the point. What I do buy is that the poet is on to something; a resonance that flows outside the individual visceral or visceral individual (however you want to look at that). The effect of language still applies.

Youssef Alaoui is no stranger to this resonance of language, and in his collection of short stories here, he has fashioned many word tapestries that function as perfect artifacts of literature.

The work envelops the reader in a variety of voices, of situations and scenarios; the tone and pitch of these words, not in how they sound (at least at first) but in how they interlock, really serve as Youssef's love letter to words themselves, to their magic. The survey made here of the human condition is wide but every note hit cuts deep and primal, on all the important scales of storytelling, and the title sequence of his sections bears this out: Urban Fables, Pastoral Fables, Missives, and Prophecies.

Within these pages, Youssef makes his own brilliant counterpoint to my cranky pseudo-atheism, successfully arguing that words are indeed sacred, and if you make it through this wild and touching ride to the point where he tells that particular story (The Alchemy of Vowels, which serves almost as a spiritual summary in the collected Prophecies) you won't particularly care what anyone's position on the subject is. You will be enthralled by the mastery of a voice that loves the cumulative power of words.

Go ahead and see for yourself. You will start on familiar, possibly even warm and comfortable ground but you will be surprised, perhaps even enthralled by where you end up. One thing you won't question is why Youssef Alaoui writes words.

-Paul Corman Roberts, author of
We Shoot Typewriters

PROEM

The stories in this book are concerned with the sociological conundrum that Buber wrote about in "I and Thou." The term thou is used to address another in a respectful manner. The term you objectifies the interlocutor. It might have been J.M. Coetzee or maybe Saussure who used the term Self vs. Foreign Other. Gayatri Chakravorty Spivak writes extensively on this relationship in regards to gender and colonialism.

This book is also about the power of the word and the failure of language, despite the magic of the letters it is composed of. Every letter of every alphabet has a historic value, a semiotic, a cultural reference, or a ritual significance for summoning elemental energy. The irony is that each letter on its own is imbued with more meaning than whole conversations or strands of letters laid out on the page. Saussure, Derrida, Barthes, Borges all wrote on the power of symbol and the ambiguity of language. Borges said ambiguity is richness. For better or worse, I believe that language is a mire.

MYSTIC SYSTEM OF THE ROSY ORDER:

STORY OF THE MAGICAL ALPHABET

Time is a model plaything dressed as the monster only we ask him to remove his makeup and looking tender at us he complies but the lights of the planet dim and air pressure increases the ghosts have found us and tear at our bodies what can one do?

ALEPH

Ox. Godhead. Cosmic Egg. The Mind. Nothing. Everything.

Does a fish type in the snow? Why do horses have buns but cows no?
Is there a god at the end of this alley because I can feel it. I have a brain
hard so tight right now on my way to meet the godhead. Electro static
resonance. Thick ropy strands of light do quiver in such a shape.

BET

House. Self. Wisdom. Mystery.

Once a lonely tower met an abandoned mineshaft. Their lovemaking was colossal and relentless. The trees swayed. The clouds cried. The sun hid. That summer they birthed a litter of rolling hills.

GIMEL

Camel. Initiate. Flow.

"The soldier is neither a boot nor a hat," said the hunchback to the one-eyed man.

Shit on concrete. Treasure in the drug heap. Lounge in soft robes. The camels recommend and wander the company of dry trees over brick and mortar jackboot rhythm—relentless flex, influx.

DAHLED

Door. Pour. Walkthrough.

The soul is a doorless door. How many rainbows deep is the quartz monument horizon? I let the blood trickle down my chin when I howl at the moon my pants down—wicked claws ripping up the air as I stand high on a rock lit by glassy lake shine.

HEH

Window. Cube of Space.

Somehow when I fold cheese, the oil based sheets of it, pressure is released in a dog's calf out in the yard where monks walk and unburden themselves for sheer recreational pleasure of sunshine under spanning fig blossoms and chipmunk bark but the waves catch each other, waves of air, playing in the sun, they catch each other and throw themselves to the ground in honest heat discussion past the brick quad I'm looking for.

Vav

Pin. Spine. Nail. Doctrine.

Fixed by a sheath of trees, rebel grass quills of the forest floor lap at the mountain crest and melt it all into sand. Suckle. Spit. Suckle. Spit. Relax. Repeat. Asana. Death. Stay behind, glow worm, for the star travels both ends of light.

ZAYIN

Sword. Lovers.

Give a gander to the drum maker: let the horn of elder beast exalt in lilting rhyme. Follow the will. When. As if you doubt the whereas. Leave the dirt droppings. This tapestry will get you nowhere. Pass the yolk that transcends rocky gates to a victorious climate of joy and beauty to be in love and to love the star of the west—the splendor and pride of thy number so strong in war, the forbidden book of stance humanity, greeting resinous cloud, sky dotted with chant.

URBAN FABLES

NIGHT WINDOW

I was aware of you dreaming and twisting, fretfully, sweatily, deep in your bed last night. Your brain pushed images from your dreams and broadcast them against the inside of your window like Balinese shadow puppets. In color.

It was you there, trapped in your covers—your forehead raked in soggy multiple Ws, beaming images which I, in turn, felt compelled to document. They were so torturous I found them cathartic.

You followed a child over a hill of golden grass, under a low drifting sun in late summer. She led you to a deep natural pool, where she drowned. We saw her submerged, vertically, eyes closed, as the bubbles stopped rising from her nostrils.

Her dress flowed, drifting slowly in the water, with long green plants growing up from the bottom. Then you were in your bed again. Your face and hair were soaking wet. It wasn't your actual bed. It was more like a crib, but your sheets were the same. Your tongue became a slug. Moist. Slender. Yellow. It crawled out of your nose to escape your anguished head. Then your eyes became two tiny blind little animals.

Your eyelids wrinkled and wept, then dissolved like paper tissue, compressing down over a million convoluted folds. This was your failing attempt to preserve that which had been so familiar, but was currently so useless. I witnessed the stress, the futility.

Your teeth were thick and yellow. So unimportant. I saw them crumble and fall out of your head like random chicken bones. The imperfect chunks rode silent streams from your mouth to the pillow.

It was at that point that the top of your head let out a babbling river of fog. No, it was more like an entire grey ocean of alphabets scribbled on wave caps pouring from nowhere and reeking of barnacles, voicing unpronounceable ancient languages and staking claim over the sleep diaries of every misshapen midnight orphan like you. It was then that your spine curled out of your back, striking the air like a scorpion's tail.

Then you rescued us with a sip of water. Your sleep had been consuming me. I yawned. I wiped my eyes. But the rain, as it tumbled from the heavens like clear blood, shredded the sheets that sudden metal soldiers had bound so tightly to protect you. The rain clawed at your face. The scratches turned into hash marks, counting every pitiful hour of endless toil you had dedicated to squirming. Then all at once you and your bed were covered in toads. They buried you and filled the window with their glaring eyes and deafening gulping noises. They slid up and down the glass with panicky muddy paws. An instant later, the window emptied. Now you're missing. Where have you gone?

Tonight, your window is black. There's little reason to stay awake, and no reason to write unless the dream was mine all along. I have decided that I must look for you tomorrow. I will keep watch on your window.

Robin With Her Eyes Closed, Running

I say these words to you dear Josh, alone in my mind, on my way to your house. I wish I was there already. Actually, I fucking hate your part of town. It's dark and gross and they don't fix the streetlights. But I'm going anyway. They towed my car. My bicycle is broken. So I have to get there on foot.

But I can shrink time when I need to, if I close my eyes and run.

The streets between my place and yours are so long and flat and boring. It's pretty easy. I just run in a straight line right through the middle of the street. Everyone parks their cars in the yard, on the rocks, on the grass. I run and close my eyes and try to think about good things, anything good—completely filling my mind with good thoughts. Running keeps me warm, too.

It's also a good time to forget. I run so hard I forget I'm passing sleeping stucco ogres pouring stale house breath out their open windows. The tiny humans inside, puffy faced and bathed in sweaty blue television light, are squished into the sofa like stinky seeds. I forget about my home and my new pit bull, curled at the foot of my couch. I miss him already. I forget how you bend me over that couch.

I remember you showing me how you masturbate, your favorite hand-grip. You make an OK circle with your finger and thumb. Then you whittle away at your helmet. You look at me and laugh when you're done—you fucking dork. You like to jerk off in public buildings too. Gas stations, the grocery, the library, the lawyer's office. Any building you've never visited before is fair game and next on the list. You said new buildings are good luck for you. Oh my god that's so lame, Josh. Isn't that against the law or something? Doesn't that legally make you a pervert?

You *are* a pervert, Josh. You're one silly mother fucker. I remember you showing me how your Native American friends taught you to dance. They might have taught you some kinda rock and roll dance but I'm sure it wasn't what you showed me. Nobody in their right mind would dance like that.

I forget about you shouting at me in front of my roommates.

I surprise myself with all the shit I can forget. It's better this way. I knew what that was, that one night, when you showed up with a gun in your pocket. You told me it was a burrito. A frozen fucking burrito. You're such a bad liar.

When I'm running I remember I am free of my roommates. I am free of their noise, their idiocy, their sloppiness, their late rent checks. I am free of my physical body. In my mind's eye, I see you smiling at me. You welcome me, with your crooked front teeth and your long wavy blonde hair. I'd say it was prettier than mine.

You've known me since I was fourteen. You were how old, twenty? But since you joined that band, and things are going better, we're sleeping together. I guess we're going out. I guess I let you fuck me. But it's more like we're friends. You're an okay friend.

Someone just lit a firecracker somewhere, a few blocks away, or maybe it's a gun. Or a bomb. That's the thing. These ogres act like they're sleeping but they're not. They're just sitting still, biding their time, waiting to let their people slip into the streets and cause mayhem. That's also why I run. Damn it, I wish I was at your place already. Street lamps pass overhead like a muddy, floating, upside-down runway.

The moon is tiny and faded tonight. And very high. I can see it through my eyelids. It looks like a bleached human skull, tilted, resting its chin at the foot of a tree.

There's a dark figure behind the tree. I can smell him. He smells like cum and sweat. I can't see his shoulders but I know he's tall and he wants me. Wants to overpower me. I run faster. My lungs burn. I can hardly catch my breath. *Please, Josh, where the fuck are you?*

My god! Someone *is* setting off bombs! I swear I heard screaming after that one! Oh Josh, won't you come meet me up the street. Oh shit shit shit where am I? This isn't your street. I must have turned wrong somewhere. Couldn't be. I only ever run straight. The streets are so fucking long and flat and wide there's no fucking way I could have taken a wrong turn. No way. There are no turns here. I feel so small . . .

Like a tiny drop of water floating past a cosmic sea of houses.

Okay. Whew. No one's chasing me. The streets are totally empty. I'm almost there. Fucking ghosts, that's what they are. Following me and fucking with my head. I need to walk to cool off a bit. Now I can see your house. There's a light on. There you are, you smug asshole, smoking on the porch. I try not to look like such a sweaty beast. I smile. "Hi."

YOUNG MIDAS

Part One: A Simple Message.

Words are but a stilted facsimile of grander concepts. Such concepts are immense thought-orchestras which do not easily lend themselves to linear reduction. For instance consider the London Philharmonic —to witness an event of this magnitude in person—the way it might envelop one's entire being at top volume, as opposed to relaying a piece of music like morse code, pecked out on a tin cup at the end of a string.

Wordlessness is bliss, and the only message of love or affection that I can send to my upstairs lover is wordless. I have never seen her, but I am certain she is female by her footsteps, by the pressure she applies to each floorboard, and by the way she gingerly makes her path to the kitchen or window. Her apartment is a mirror of mine.

The only means to proclaim my desire, strange as it may seem, is through the dark space of my bathroom window. We share a ventilation shaft. We have been granted, by miracle of architecture, this sound portal through which to convene. We have derived much pleasure from our relationship, never needing to meet yet always wanting to listen. It is obvious to me, because I can tell by the way she dallies at the doorway of her bathroom.

Likewise, I can tell she misses me every time she leaves by her pattern of footsteps. She makes a direct line, then a parry, sometimes leans into the bathroom for a moment, and slams the door on exiting. I find this jarring at times but I am tolerant of most things.

Our conversations began like this: For years she cooked and creaked and bathed and cleaned and, as it happened on the 4th of January of this year, after I peed at about 1PM, I noticed her moaning and gasping in the throes of passion. The sound was unmistakable. Disarmed, half nude, clutching myself, I was struck by the realization that I had somehow just cooperated in a sexual act.

I believe she found the sound of my urinating not only desirable, but erotic. This would be our first ecstatic union.

Since that time, and feeling yet a bit acrophobic for having already scored so well without knowing the precise detail, I have devised a method. If I feel there is an adequate amount to be brought forth, I am in the habit of projecting it at the depth of the bowl, to demonstrate the length and power of my member. I create a thick and steady stream with a bold tone I am sure will resonate through the air shaft.

In addition, I will not flush before several healthy ending squirts which, I am hoping, will convey the volume of energy bundled in my body. I am certain this pleases her, for her habits remain the same.

She prefers to make love to me in the afternoon, for that is the hour of her bath. She draws the water and takes her time to soak, then tiptoes to her closet, and lets the water flow down the side of my wall, through the pipes which whistle meandering lullabies only she and I know are special.

Life is good this way, and we are sweet to one another. At times

I find myself chuckling in my sleep. At night, I dream of her presence above me as an afghan crocheted by a grandmotherly goddess. The afghan is a womb with an umbilical cord to the cosmos, aglow in hues of red, pink, and blue.

Yes an afghan made just for us, imbued with warmth and love. It is so large it wraps twice around the walls of our apartments, and we are twins, aloft in a bi-level uterine cube, cruising the vast realms of sleep, over and under, side by side, hand in hand.

Part Two: I Got Your Message

One day, I receive a telephone call. A female voice, nervous and determined: "I've got the remote to your stereo."

"You what? You . . .why . . .whatever for?"

"I told the building manager about the situation and he let me in to grab your remote. Others have complained. He figured it was the easiest way to solve the problem. Better than kicking you out. Now I will just shut your ass down if you keep blasting that classical music of yours."

"When can I have it back?"

"You can't. Go buy a universal or something. I can't handle your shit anymore so I am going to keep it up here. And don't start blasting your TV either. I know you don't now, so thank you in advance, but just try to respect your neighbors, okay? No loud noise after 10PM. That's the rule.

And shut your bathroom window too 'cause even with mine shut, that noise—it just travels up and you seem to have this perverse enjoyment you get from pissing or something. Well, that's gross, you know? So cut it the fuck out.

You're also a compulsive throat clearer. It's annoying. I think I can even hear you laughing by yourself in your sleep late at night. It's kind of creepy.

Sound travels, you know? Also, I'm sorry if this sounds rough, but my boyfriend is ready to come down and discuss things with you if we can't arrive at some sort of agreement or something . . . Hey! Are you listening?"

I hang up the phone, utterly shocked and disoriented. She has a boyfriend. She's seeing someone else. I shut all my windows and lower the drape over the main one, facing the street. The following months are going to be cold.

Part Three: When Summer is Cold, Autumn is a Relief

Time, under duress, expresses itself as *duration*. The time it takes to close a window. The time it takes to scrub a pan. The number of minutes it takes for a shadow to travel down a building. But, time is also *tedium*. How much longer must I wait for her? Do they really love one another? In the end, time is only *delirium*.

In my delirium, the future is erased, the past lingers, and the present is infinite, only to be hacked at in tiny measured paces. It is unbearable. The bit-by-bit procedures that comprise my workdays kill me at every moment. They have shrunk to a circuit of repetitive physical movements, which, in turn, hypnotize my brain, so I am alive, but numb. A clockwork idiot. Minute phrases form at the core of my body. I am victim to three self-effacing mantras:

She's-Gone-Now.
Lover-Come-Back.
I-Am-Dead.

At home, my symphonies are all I can lose myself in. At precisely ten, my stereo is snapped off, sometimes at seven. But I can still use my headphones. At least they are more sufficient than tin cans. They collect salt rings from the sheer distress that leaks out my eyes in the pit of night.

My cosmic afghan has been snapped away from me. I find myself spinning in a cold, dark starless expanse, suspended by a wire within the gloom of a dead warehouse in my mind, where a factory floor may have been, currently laden with dust. The only illumination trickles through a skylight window piled with bird shit. I haven't the strength to lift my head to inspect the final borders of my prison.

My limbs hang like butchered legs of lamb. My palms and eyebrows raise themselves to the sky, as if fish-hooked to wayward balloons. But the one thought, the one that really twists the knife in my gut, is to know that all this could easily have been worse.

Part Four: Homecoming

Tonight is Friday. I shut myself in at 7:30PM and am asleep by 9:00. Curiously however, in a kind of walking dream, I find myself wandering my apartment looking for music. Which album, I can't be sure. Reading is difficult. I notice the apartment is oppressive with shadows. The air is hot and thick. So very strange.

I feel jolts of electricity all over my skin. My footsteps feel very light on the floor. The muscles in my legs beg to bound, but fearing I might hit my head on the ceiling, I skip instead. I moonwalk laps around my bedroom and living room.

Suddenly I am in the main hallway where I discover a game to play. There is a banister bolted to the wall at the far end. It is part of the staircase. I find that I am so light I can climb above it and perch, with my feet against the wall. I grip the banister and squat above it. There is an old motel painting on the wall knocking me off balance, so I kick it aside. I spring off and then discover that I can swim and flail to stay aloft. I can fly the entire hallway like this. I try it several times. My head is dizzy and my heart is aglow. I wander the hallway effortlessly, bouncing, bumping off walls and ceilings, closing and opening my apartment door. Now, to rest, I drift inside, when I notice something wet under my foot.

I float to place my chest on the carpet. It is a footprint! A small flurry of them. Coming from the bathroom and leading to the closet. This couldn't be her apartment. Am I upstairs? Surely not. She has come to visit me. But why?

Why? Because this is a dream. My dream! And here, we are perfect. Here, she pads her wet feet in MY apartment. She promises herself to ME and I accept her, under any circumstance. This thought releases me. I kick to the air and bellow a noiseless sleep howl. My throat buzzes. My chest resonates. I am dancing, floating air circles with the old remote to my stereo in my hands again, at last.

I cry with elation. Tears fly from my head in slow silver drops. They sparkle in the shadows. It is all too much to behold. Falling to the floor, I realize I am wiping my eyes with a smooth woman's nightie. I fold it neatly, kindly, and amble into bed.

Thunder Brings Me Two Memories

If you don't cry, it isn't love
If you don't cry,
then you just don't feel it deep enough.
— Magnetic Fields, "69 Love Songs"

Tonight the sky pulses with thunder. I am wracked with visions of our sweaty voyage down my living room carpet. "You fucked me across the floor," you declared, with sweat collected in the folds of your chest, eyes glowing, half-closed.

"We wha...?" I think about how I told you on our hike that I was a *version of a virgin*. "Hang on, I gotta change a tire," and we continued. Because you brought us Chianti at a quarter to ten. Because you were nervous about your upcoming trip.

Because you fear love. Because you fear you'd fall out of love. You won't let yourself have deep feelings for others. I believe it's vanity. I believe you have damned yourself.

Because you did not kiss me hello. Because I remember

everything. Because I'll always remember how you danced to the music I played for you the night before. "This is YOU? You did that?"

"Yes, I did that. Why is that so—" And you pulled me up by my arms and we danced to the music I recorded with my old band. We played so perfectly together. We each composed our own parts, never treading on another's moment to shine. No arguments. No bullshit. I still use that band as a reference for what any great relationship can be. Disaster struck our band. A disaster too ordinary to be mentioned here.

"You fucked me across the floor!" you laughed. And I had. We slid a good six feet from where we'd started. There was more to follow.

You clutched me like a starfish. You sipped wine from my cocoon. You saw me in a way that others won't. Your public was your life. You touched people for work. You called to them in your mind, and they would appear.

At no time had you met one so promising, so present, as me. For that, you are grateful. For that, I am grateful. I saw you immediately as a fleeting gift. I knew you would leave as easily as you came. I will miss your graciousness, generosity, health, and beauty. You were certain that life would always offer you great choices. I wonder how that turned out for you.

You said you had never been hurt in love. You liked to kiss and tell. You asked me, "What was the greatest sex you've ever had?"

And I said, "Well," sparing you the details, "once, in the snow."

"In the snow!" you cooed.

"And once was with the *London Times*."

"The newspaper?"

I couldn't respond. The memories of a stay at the London Hilton flew to the front of my mind. A series of experiments in alcohol, gluttony, room service, a pill, and bestial positioning welled up and competed with the sensuous body laid out before me.

"Wow we've been at it for two hours now!" I said.

But you were not swayed from your topic. If not hearing tales of sexual pleasure, you will tell them. With all the details. "Once I was giving this boy head . . ."

"Mm-hmn . . ." I looked down. I couldn't help but imagine. All young men to you are *boy*.

"Once, this boy and I were frying on acid, in the rain, on a prairie. I was giving him head, and right as he came, thunder rang out in the sky." You were amazed with yourself. "We were under a blanket. It was really incredible. Too bad he turned out to be . . . not so good."

Tonight, thunder blasts in deafening peals overhead. It shakes the walls of the room where we cuddled. Rain cools the city and flows over streets we walked together. I no longer want to own the contents of my head. I would rather give it all up to charity. Maybe someone else in the world wants my surplus visions in their collection, for pleasure or permanent disposal. For now, thunder brings me two memories. One mine, one yours.

ELVIS, KING OF CATS

Been face up to the rain for an hour or more this early morning. My cot is tight around my elbows. My window is a clear plastic square framed in aluminum, cut right into a roof that slants sharply down one wall of my tiny room, which used to be a maid's quarters. The window is held open by its closure. I can barely reach my head through, but when I do, all the rooftops of Paris are splayed out in front of me like a medieval etching. I watch the rain and imagine I am inside it. The liquid silver squeezes out of puffy floating dragons, silent, sliding, some bluer than others, creating puddles in the streets deep enough to strand a car.

I live in a quarter called *Amérique*, in the 19th arrondissement, so of course I call myself an American. It is close to the Place des Grandes Rigoles, off the Rue des Pyrénées. *Rigoles* are laughs and *Pyrénées* are mountains. Life here should be a rollicking laugh-a-minute romp, as I jump from mountaintop to mountaintop, but guess what—*Rigoles* refers to ditches and *Pyrène* is the name of a young woman who was raped by the drunken cow-thieving Hercules, on one of his missions. These are *her* mountains. Paris placed the street of Pyrène's mountains next to the laughing ditches. In fact, this area is shunned by most of Paris. *I will not walk down those streets by day or by night!* they say. Really, we are all Africans here: *Maghrebins.*

France occupied Algeria and made protectorates of Morocco and Tunisia. They came. They conquered. They left. Now we're left with a few street names and some trucks rusting in the sand. Once we get to France, with higher hopes, we live like this, and I live off the tiny park of ditches, next to the inebriated, conquering grasp of Hercules. But never mind him. He's a leader of the catastrophe, and I am Elvis, King of Cats.

A little song jumps into my head for an otherwise grim morning:

> *But I'm good, okay*
> *and "so what" they say*
> *y'know I'm ready to slay*
> *because I am the starchy grin*
> *tin can raider and never mind*
> *the criminal man!*
>
> *I am Elvis, King of Cats!*
>
> *Yeah I fly around the roundabouts*
> *on my black motorbike "Pépé le Moto"*
> *Beep-beep, you jerk!*
> *Pesky for you, clean escape for me.*
>
> *I am Elvis, King of Cats!*
>
> *I head straight for the mad gangs*
> *of pigeons and away they fly*
> *frantic razor cloud in the air*
> *flyin' and divin' their "upandaways"*

upandaways!
upandaways!

Damn, you fool pigeons
why settle down in the same place
you know I'm comin' back!
No park is safe! Ima come find ya!

I am Elvis, King of Cats!

Right on. A song is born. I'm staring into my eyeball and a dream comes back at me through the mirror. I dreamt that I lost my eyes but that I could still see, and someone had bought me fake ones and an applicator. I sat on the floor and looked at the applicator, a long plastic tube. I looked at the eyeballs—one was looking back at me and the other was looking off in its own direction. I thought, *there's no way I'm going to be able to put that eyeball into my head without some help, and, how will my eyelid wrap around that THING and should I suck on the eyeball first and then pop it in?*

It came to me that my eyes were vulvas and these eyeballs were face babies. My waking mind mulls over this as I smooth-comb my jet black pompadour. Glass eyes would be more like foster babies, wouldn't they? Are eyelids labia? Are eyeballs reborn every time we blink? Or is it *reality* that is reborn? What if our environment is potentially refreshed every time we blink, and all of reality is reborn when we wake from sleep? Sleep would be a chance to regroup, to forgive, to forget, and therefore death would be a complete reset and renewal.

No breakfast. There's no food here anyway. I have a tiny fridge. It holds a crusty chunk of butter and a quarter jar of mustard. I am through with eating. Most food makes me ill in one way or another. I am . . .undersized. Let's just say that I live on black leather and pomade. *My pomp is long and circumstances are short*, is what I tell myself. I keep a little radio tuned to a station that plays American oldies all day long. I mispronounce words, or rather, my words come out malformed due to a minor stroke I had in my twenties, which prohibited me from full-time work. Part of my tongue is immobile. The government pitched in for a while. I was on medical leave. Soon after, I was enlisted part-time for a regional civic project to protect and feed feral cats. Then the government abolished the program, but most people still know me in that capacity. I like it. I get donations of kibble from friends, and once in a while a butcher will give me a scrap or two, but I must be careful. A woman was recently fined over 500 euros for feeding cats.

It is twelve levels down to the street from my tiny pad under the roof. Once for a maid, now, La Casa de Funk. I've got this thing dialed—James Dean, Bogart, Brando, a still from *Wild Bunch*, Bukowski, and a little typewriter for all my daydreams on a two-by-three desk built into the wall, hanging over the foot of my bed. For my place, getting upstairs can be a chore, but going down is a calculated breeze. It's a lotta stairs with one continuous wooden oval bannister snaking down the whole way, propped by a fence of iron bars. A lesson in perspective.

I kick my little black *Pépé le Moto* into action. Outta here. Down the way. Rue des Rigoles. Pass the Père LaChaise, where they finished off the Communards. Burnin' down the Roquette on my way to the Bastille. How many people have died by the side of this road? *Depot of the Condemned*, they called the prison on Roquette. Paris whips by me as I tuck and dive between cars, bicycles, and pedestrians. I lean into the turns at corners and roundabouts. I shoot at the pigeons with my finger. I downshift with *Pépé* and work my way past a delivery truck that blocks my view. Rockin' and rollin'. Cruisin' and bruisin'. I stop by the butcher to see what he has for the kitties today. Oh yeah, he has saved a little treat. Now back to the grid: the mangled network of streets and tributaries of Paris is a sardonic monument to colonialism and medieval despair, as well as a passing commemoration of ingenuity.

Burgundy massacre of 1418. Marie Antoinette. Robespierre. Danton. Revolutions of blood. Napoleon. Haussmann. Revolutions of stone and blocks. Paris is constantly washed in the blood of its people. Buildings are blown up or pulled down to make way for the new. The mine was cut deeper for building materials. Then Paris dug up the dead and stacked them in fastidious piles, creating a labyrinth of the dead. The fumes of death permeate up through moist and glittering concentric pavers. Sorbonne students dug the pavers out with their bare hands and threw them at police in '68.

I pass Boulevard Voltaire. Up to my right is the *Bataclan*. I continue to Rue St. Antoine, Fourcy, Ile Saint Louis, Pont Saint Louis. Notre Dame Cathedral is the pupil of Paris. The *périphérique* outlines the eye. Structure, rupture, rubble, displacement, replacement. As I speed down the streets, I can almost feel them being ripped up to the sky in my wake, pavers flying, dirt exposed, tree roots, baby carriages, rabble and revolutions, pedestrians in black, all flying upward because Paris must blink to refresh her reality, wetting her streets with the blood of her people. I can feel a blast and glass showers from every corner restaurant. People cross the street in a hunker, as if they too are ducking.

The sky clears. I park my bike and stare at the back side of Notre Dame. She has furry spider legs and a chambered abdomen. She was here when Paris was still connected by foot paths, when Saint Germain was really a prairie. She watched the whole city begin. She witnessed the infamous cat massacre of Saint Severin.

This park has a few trees, little green benches that are sublime in the sunshine, and orange gravel everywhere. The kitties come running. I have fresh ground chicken heart in my pocket. They don't care. There is a situation. Behind the cathedral, by the fence, behind a bench, there is a tiny hole. I think they want me to hunt for rabbits with them. I get down and start digging. They wait in anticipation. A small crowd of tourists collects around me. I widen the hole and pull out a little kitten. Her mother takes her by the neck and crates her off. I find another kitten. A different cat picks that one up. I pick out a final tiny kitten, and the mother is back to carry this one off. Relief. The cats will eat their snacks now . . . such a little drama. The crowd claps. They offer me money. I take a few bucks and bow. I am aware of police looking on. I say *thank you, thank you very much.* Just then a rabbit bounds out of the hole and the cats run after it. It is all gone in a blur of fur, whiskers, and plumes of dust.

I walk *Pépé* to the Latin Quarter. Rue de la Huchette. Little asshole is low on fuel. They do not sell gas around here. Here where I post fliers I make for bands. This is the street of smashed plates, the tiny street of meat roasters, the street famous for jazz. Everyone likes my fliers—the heads of the musicians are suspended in a field of black ink. They're cheap but it gets the point across.

I park *Pépé* and someone taps me on the shoulder. A heavily-armed young soldier asks me for my name. I tell him I am Elvis, King of Cats. He says he needs my real name. I tell him my real name. He asks for my papers. I have nothing on me, *everyone knows me.* I say I have papers at home. *Who are you,* they ask again. I tell them again who I am. They search my pockets. They find blood on my hand from the chicken heart. They whisk me to the station and shut me in a back room.

What they say is ridiculous. I demand to see my representative. They laugh. They tell me to open my bag. I have a small backpack. They want me to empty my pockets. I have a few pockets, they are empty. I have cat food. I have the remains of a chicken heart and blood in my pocket. They exchange looks of curiosity and disgust, then order me to take off my clothes. I take off my shirt. I am shouting. They are smiling. I am horribly skinny like a small camel. *Mouse camel.* My buttocks look like a camel's hoof. That is how Herman Hesse described Siddhartha Gautama. I am the Parisian street buddha. I am not the Algerian drug hustler they think I am. They order me to turn around. I turn my back to them. They have me spread my cheeks apart. My stomach is sick. They grab me by the neck and lower my head. They put one of my legs up on a chair so that I am fully exposed. They tell me to cough. I do not cough. They insist. I cough. I hear a door open. There is a man two rooms back, peering into my backside from his desk. I do not understand. *Cough,* they say all at once. I cough.

I tell them they will hear from my representative. They laugh at me. They take me to a holding cell and throw my clothes at me. It's ironically larger than my apartment. I am released a few hours later. My bag and my jacket are lying on a table. They have opened everything stitch by stitch. My backpack and every tiny part is spread across a large table. My jacket is in shreds. It looks like ribbons. They escort me to the street. I put my jacket on defiantly and zip it up although the back twirls open. I can get *Pépé* later, they say.

I am resting back at the apartment, toying with the radio. I stick my head out the window, gazing at the streets below me. I find a new station playing a bizarre song. I crank it:

> *Eternal city of mud*
> *I hear you calling my name*
> *from your crusty roofs to the pit of your station.*
> *I'm awash in your crowds and I'm searching for food.*

But if your streets are a jungle
then I must be a coward.
Your animals bray in the thick summer night.
I hear the fur of your skin, the teeth in your skull.
Where your streets collide I am treading the walls . . .

I put on my old brown coat and feed the cats in the Place des Grandes Rigoles. Little bastards don't know what happened today. I am thinking about taking that walk, finally, in the allées south of Rue de Mouzaïa. They say there is an *Allah* written in the streets. It is a walking route. Pedestrians follow a route to trace the word *Allah*. Walker as pen. Hm. Tonight I will see for myself.

. . . I'm getting dressed in the late night
to follow you home.
Pasting down my hair so I can lure you in.
Brittle moon high above
a black frozen pond . . .

On my way, I see a large, long-haired, glowing white cat. She sees me too, and I follow. We are running down the streets, in the direction of the *Allah*. I am excited to see what this is about. The streets of Paris do not only recall history, but by their proximity to one another, they comment on it. This section of streets forms a Roman temple, with a spire, the Rue de Fraternité, that points up to the star intersection of the Métro Danube. It leads down to the peak of the roof, Rue de la Liberté and Rue de L'egalité. Villa du Progrès is the main support beam in the center of the roof. Rue de Mouzaïa forms the base of the roof and completes the triangle.

. . . I hear the radio on. It tells me what to say.
Bleeding dawn on the pavement, now you're leading me on.
Between the towers of clay, you put your good friend down.
Flood it deep and wide under a mouthy shine . . .

Mouzaïa is the name of a city in Algeria. The Paris code of the streets has "crowned" Mouzaïa with *Liberté*, *Fraternité*, and *Egalité*. South of the roof is a special section of walkways called "villas." These are as columns for the temple. The Roman temple sits on a street called Bellevue: *beautiful vista*. This is so ironic that I am smiling again, as I approach the small pilgrimage.

. . . You're all over the pavement you crazy thing.
Moving towers of clay and an antique smile . . .

I am contra sense. I must run up to Rue de Mouzaïa and find the Villa des Lilas. Lilacs seem innocent enough. I must run south, in the direction of the first calligraphic stroke. Aha. I see a small golden tile pressed into the plaster at eye level, midway on the wall. ALIF: *Allah*. I run to Rue de Bellevue. Then I take Villa Sadi Carnot . . . oh no, who was that? Master of explosions! I return to Rue de Mouzaïa. There are tiny mirrors embedded in the wall, indicating HAMZA: *Lion heart. Brave. Strong. Fair.* I must walk a loop. Then Villa de Bellevue. LAM: *Benevolent.* It is connected to the next LAM. On Emile Loubet, midway down, there is mist and rain. The glowing cat is at the end of the alley, across the Rue Mouzaïa. I must follow. SHADDA: *Female twins. Fragrance of flowers.* I see the mirrors. I tap them. Crumbs of plaster fall. I walk in two semicircles. It feels like dancing. I move my arms. I see an arrow on the sidewalk pointing north, to the St. Francis of Assisi church. Why the church? The glowing cat is up ahead. Behind the church, in the middle of a blank wall, are painted six small blue daggers, no more than three inches high. Almost unnoticeable, but I see them. Why. Why? Dagger ALIF, the sixth stroke of the writing of the name Allah, praised be his name! Of course! Are the Catholics complicit with this walking route? Saint Francis of Assisi accepted all humans, all animals.

> *. . . There's no cure for appeal*
> *when all you ever do is shine.*

I hear muffled screams. It is Hercules and Pyrène, again. His hands are made of mist. They slide into her clothing. He will make her famous unless I stop this madness. I grab a bent umbrella from the trash and run at him. His back is enormous. I hit and hit it, and the coat falls empty onto Pyrène. No, it is not her. It is the glowing cat. I have killed her.

I must look for the final stroke of Allah. The letter HA. *Truth.* Where in this city is truth? How did the cat get under a coat? I am in tears. I go on my way. The route for HA forces me to enter one building, go out the back door, and come back through another building. There is a doorman at the second building. He says good evening. I say nothing. He says it again. I turn and nod. He looks at me, sees my face, my long pompadour and sideburns, my old coat. I run. He runs after me. He calls for police. I run down the Rue des Rigoles. My footsteps ricochet off the buildings like disembodied laughter. He has dropped off. I hear sirens, but Paris is full of hee-hawing sirens and I am very tired. It is time to end this. I make it to my tiny room. I take off my wet layers but keep my tee shirt on and put on my soft flannel pajama bottoms. I need to sleep, to reset, and even, perhaps to forgive. When I am reborn, I know I will be a country as yet unnamed.

Two Bits

1. *The Blockhouse, Central Park, Manhattan.*

Manhattan has had indigestion for over two hundred years, consuming and belching out humans and culture since before this country was born. What started as a hiccup has matured into a complex, gassy, multi-chambered stomach of wrought iron and concrete. The streets are intestines. Holland tunnel, the asshole. Central Park, the lungs, is where I now sit. I can see the city breathing in front of me, moving in the trees. The American flag is an uvula. It purrs occasionally atop its pole, way overhead.

~⁓

Over eight million souls cramped into 22.82 square miles, but it's not difficult to find yourself alone on this island. Truth is, you most often are. Manhattan is a lonely-human-making machine.

Thousands of ships and planes are drawn to these shores. The city summons, in one way or another, every object and every human on the planet. One might estimate that, roughly speaking, at least two representatives of every country of the world are here, at all times, on any street corner, in any five block radius. Likewise, any act, any procession, ritual, or procedure humanly possible is currently or will soon take place in the space of a single day on this city island. If it can be conceived by the human brain, you can bet it is happening right now or will occur at some point today in Manhattan, including the setting of my butt on a lawn, by myself, on a sunny day, next to the blockhouse, in a park, listening to the flag wave overhead, notebook in hand.

⁓

What of this city? What is its reflection? All this nonsense writing about nonsense, uttering more nonsense and then—what? Look, my block letters are city blocks, dressed in alphabet cloak and numerically designated paragraphs. At the core of my imagination is a park, a lung, filtering thought pollution, expanding and contracting, and trapped in place by a skull of civic barnacles and random movement. The intent is to be here, now. What I tend to do is stare down at the page and become aware of my inky soul slipping out the point of my pen and flattening into the handheld spiral bound stack of bleached leaflets. I am surprised at just how empty a soul can be. How many hashmarks will it take for me to commit it to paper—the memory of autumn colors, a street dog and *Yoo Hoo*, my eyes opening to the breezes in this park? We shall see.

II. *Front Porch Sunset, Tucson, Arizona.*

Now here's a blank page that beckons. This dusty cushion is the true score. Street-found flop-couch. God knows where it's been but who gives a shit—I'm only here for a few days. Yep, the desert is raw and quiet.

Last night a 23-year-old little missy taught us how to shoot the pool ball straight. She'd been learning for just under a year herself. She promised us that once she gets that handgun she will not hesitate to shoot it. In self-defense only, of course. Says she played with snakes and javelinas as a child before the tiny spot of Marana, Arizona, was even a spot.

Marana is a town today. I've seen it. The bus from Phoenix stopped at an adobe liquor store in Marana. That's where those two women got on. One of them went straight to the toilet. The other, a blonde, sat behind me. Opposite row. Wore glasses. I felt a beam from her face for the rest of the ride. I think she might have wanted a little conversation.

This paper is yanking useless lines of ink out of my pen. I can't put anything worthwhile down and yet the pen won't stop. I feel the moment ending. M returns. N and T are finished practicing. The four of us converge on the front porch. Speaking that Frenchy thing. It's good. French is a language meant to be whispered. Sort of a pouty, mushy little language, somehow massaging syllables . . .

Voom. Right back to a similar moment. Déja vu. M comes up the step and through the door and that's about it. T and N never reappear. I hear their voices over the wall of the porch. The paper is still here in my hands.

This thirsty little pad is demanding to be lubricated with ink. A fly licks my finger. The low afternoon sun lights its abdomen like an amber bead. My toes are numb from crossing my legs. A woman across the street mumbles at her children. She laughs now and then, then voices sternly at the dog. The freeway swishes. A distant dog yelps. The sun resigns. The breeze lightens. The leaves jostle. A car passes, brakes whistling. Most brakes do here, from dirt in the drums. Flies wander and probe. The trunk of a car squeaks. Its lid responds to pits in the dusty street. The walls soak sound. The neighbor paints. My note pad beckons. Dishes clank and crash inside. My stomach would feign hunger at this moment, but responds as if sunburnt. Bushwhacked.

⁓

Here in desert land, the people are still, yet moving. Active, yet sticky. Sore, yet grateful. Well-behaved, yet inefficient. Thoughtful, yet brave. Innocent, yet reticent. Everyone ready. The sun lowers. The trees jostle. The horizon pulls wind toward it. The air leans to embrace the sun. The neighbor lights a pipe. Marijuana most likely. Might be thinking of offering. M's voice nears the door and fades back to her room. She's speaking English. N approaches the screen door. Light decreases in quanta. The breeze continues. The ocean is far. The mountain bathes in thick yellow light. Stomach groans. Sun dips below a roof. Hank Williams creeps out the door. Mood changes. Good night, goodbye. I will watch the rest of this sunset without words.

PASTORAL FABLES

This is How the Story Goes

This is exactly how the story goes. This is how it rang like a firefly in the corners of church houses and dormitories. Here is what they said to one another for three millennia, shouted from the backs of camels, spoken with the eyes through peepholes in backyard walls. Here is the story as the people told it to one another over dinner and late nights, charming the tangerine moons, all honey and butter in gentle summer wind.

There once was born, in a tiny village, not so far away, a very young man with an extremely short left leg which may not have presented such a problem had his right leg not been so superhumanly long. For many years he scuttled it behind him like fleshy refuse, yelling at the air, saying, "this pond is inopportune lollygagging! Time has cut mustard sauce in half with you! Window dried salty figurines!" And the people passed and followed their routines, for in his age, the streets were filled with places to go and more things to think about than just bread and clean water.

The very young man had lanterns in the imagination which gave way to foggy streets or sunshine spires, with each step so fretfully impeding his journey through town. His father and mother worried not, for their concern was bicycle repair in the closets of clients with full gardens and lace in the window. But his troubles were troubling and the questions arose yet the others never bothered, so he inquired within.

Within, he heard knocking. A rattling like footsteps. Perhaps the clumsy tap-dance of a proprietor, but who owned the interior? Maybe the chairs skidded backward and the horns blared in frustration, but the heat never left and the clouds kept on building. Yes, he yelled in consequence: "Torn gullets and water creatures! The tortoise never appears! Only the lake valley yawns and stares at the girdle, a fish, a bear, the jackal in underwear, popcorn science and stolen quilts made of lollipops. I have eggs in my pocket, damned if I use them. Chicanery is kindness! The healing dogs touch throughout my heart. I must learn to leap!"

The very young man then closed his eyes deep. His misty towels at the shelter were distributed among the service and hobbled on their way back down to the yard, to bake in the sun before the thunderstorms arrived.

Meanwhile, perhaps a somebody no one looked on in curiosity but then lowered her chin as if asking the spirit to render her pregnant from her work with the sheets on the bed in the room on the farm in the middle of the times when visitors passed and gave up their thanks at the table, laden with teas and cakes of the forefathers, diagonal beams falling from the window, cleansing the plates and shooting the ceiling.

Breakfast of black cocoa and water, a skinless banana. Books that spread like confetti, the children of pages. Amusement frames ticking slowly by, through drapes and soft music. Alliances confusing. Somewhere from the mud came up a bubble and then all was static. The toy horse of reason. Moth in a flame. Molten saliva. Sky weeps responding.

The very young man had everything determined. His walking straight fancy and vanilla windmills recorded. His outsides were flopping and his innards milked snake fangs. The windowless walls looked down in amusement. Buildings behind street lamps leaned in to support him. Anywhere would he go with impulses flaring, to brave new moons and a crusty horizon. Either explore or perish. This was determination.

So for days he disassembled mattresses in far rooms of the household. Mother and father away on their work-horsing. And of them he built a crust with a balloon at the center, some carved marble and sweet crackers with gangway planks, chandeliers, and snowy down layers among them. Of gold and silver he spun and spun a nest so deep, the caverns held darkness with full sun splitting over. Bridges he wrought, with towers that carried shoulders of flag wrapped heroes. Here he was nestled in the core of his bosom, on a settling sky, a midnight couch. It was the hermit pause. Spirit doze.

And on one morning, his mind was reborn. Games traced in dirt lit up like the chalkboard of a sunroom. Emergence of plaster walls sopped with unreason and disbelief. Sagging flowers on paper, sun on the land. The moist stress of rebirth. Here lay fortune. First step as a man, nude, plausible, erect, right leg as tremendously long as it ever was, left leg curiously stumpy. But yet in the now was his skull both rolled back and absorbent. Now ready, walk in princely manner, completely painted elder master hunter collector washboard bender royal stepper holy roller. His first coup counted so extremely much to the lay-awake world in its fervent ever-roundness, prim streets jutting at the edges, sprouted pudgy babies laughing and loving mothers chest fanning.

The bicycle pedestrians parted like the wake of a ferry driving clear waters bound for sandy shores of foreign islands, trees baking in air, horses scurrying to a hole in the building. Sunned roofs of his village shone like wheat field grasses blowing clay beds that tighten, where ancient jungles flatten, exposing jeweled beauty marks and clear rivers. And from there, the very young man telegraphed his works, rolling through the streets of his town, sharing purest form, saying "these succulent pearls come from clouds cut like dried tears. Share, love, proliferate. Live, alive, give, forgive. We are now cloud collaboration Eliyahu."

And the tale spun on for centuries, whipping like leopards foraging deep underwater, dancing the branches of linden maidens, fancy-free and taffeta-turning for hours, sparkling flame tops, chimneys in the walls, hanging gardens of Babylon, like water through towns laying drunk on light pressed flat by the baking sky. At last pain moratorium. Forests of castles shook to the rhythm of purity steps taken from this point onward, exactly as the story goes, for the very young man with his flexible beating heart of newborn acceptance.

The Story of Furry Animals
And How They Came To Be That Way

Oh my god, dad, stop it—you're ruining my eggs! That's too much! You poured salsa everywhere!

Don't worry little dude, just mix it and you'll be fine! Besides, you know what they say, don't you?

What, that *dads should not mess with the plates of their children especially when they are in that kid's favorite breakfast spot when he is finally staring down a plateful of huevos y papas cuando el papi es un loco en su cabeza?*

Calm down. No that's not what they say. They say that a good salsa will put hair on your chest!

What if I don't want hair on my chest? Especially not from eating these huevos y papas. That would suck if when I got home after soccer and took a shower and saw hair sprouting out of my chest. You know, I would come looking for you, papi!

Hahaha! Silly boy. I understand. You have my permission to come looking for me. But anyway, what I wanted to tell you about was the story of furry animals and how they came to be that way.

Aw, man! Is this another one of your shaggy dog tales?

Well, this one literally is, but actually is not.

What? Well, go ahead but keep your hands off my plate.

Long ago, before there were very many humans, before they found fire or forged hammers or dreamt up castles or jails or war, animals walked the earth in exquisite comfort, each suited to their particular environment by means of their body shape and size. This system worked fine for millions of years. They needed no fur. During the day they would do their creaturely activities and then stretch out in the sun to warm themselves and relax.

At night, they would come down from the trees and come in from the field to hang out with one another, every sort of animal, to share stories, to share the finer points of their day, and to fend off the chill of the night. The animals' skin was marvelous to behold. Some were bright pink, some had black and white splotches, and some were translucent; their red and blue veins showed through their skin very easily. The pile of animals in all their hues, in their comfortable rumbling chatter, was a beautiful sight.

One day, the weather changed. They found it uncomfortable to make their creaturely rounds during the day but still found warmth together every evening. Then it got colder and it stayed cold. The animals found it unbearable to make their rounds. They took to grouping up all day on the forest floor, huddled against their favorite rock. They told stories of when it was warmer, what the bees were doing, what color the flowers were. Some went hungry because they refused to leave the others to go foraging.

A few died. This made the pile of animals colder. It was a sad time. They said goodbye to their friends and pushed them far away from the heap. That night, they noticed two round, red eyes glaring at them from the perimeter of the woods. "Who are you?" they yelled, but there was no answer. The eyes walked in a circle, in the dark, around the poor chilly animals huddled on the forest floor. Their good days were gone. Their friends were dying, and a stranger was leering at them.

"Allow me to introduce myself." It was a tall, noble, muscular, shaggy chihuahua dog who came peeking through the trees. "I come from a land very far south where it is still warm, but it is a mountainous country so we need this stuff all over our skin to protect us when we forage our magical diet, high in the mountains. We call it FUR!" The animals in a pile did not move from where they were but they did say "Oooh" and "Ahhh" as they marveled at the dog's commanding stature and thick rolls of fur.

"What we do is mix up a magical batch of salsa. Salsa just means *sauce*. We make the sauce in several ways. We eat it on our food or we even eat it by itself when we want the pure power. Salsa is an amazing and flavorful combination of vegetables and once you try it you will find it is *muy picante* or *very hot*. It has an internal heat that will give you warmth throughout the cold days. There is a field not far from here where the ingredients grow together naturally. I will take you there in the morning!"

This chihuahua dog was obviously a shaman. The cold and starving creatures had been all over the area but never saw any magical plants growing in the field but they didn't know what one would look like, unless they were shown. Truly this was a powerful visitor. His sauce must be the reason for his strength and vigor. They were curious. Tomorrow would surely be an amazing day. But who would go with him? Nobody wanted to go.

The chihuahua went out early the next morning. He had little need for sleep. He had helped other animals on his pilgrimage north from home. The premise for his pilgrimage was simple: he would walk until he found suffering. These days it was not difficult.

He would walk for five months and back again, helping whomever he could along the way.

Today, he would check the field for his new friends. He had seen some of the good plants growing in a patch of sun. He had a good feeling about this. He looked for hours. Then he checked some familiar looking places. He did not see the spot he noticed the day before. He would look elsewhere. Nothing. He found other plants and food for the others. He brought back what he could. They eagerly lapped up what he had brought them.

"Is this salsa?"

"No. It is not. I will try again tomorrow."

The animals looked at each other and doubted his power. They murmured quietly together in their calico pile of skin tones: blue, brown, pink, and translucent with all the blood veins exposed. Doubt came quick to them. They had been in steady decline for some time. They watched him curl up and fall asleep on his own, a few yards away.

"We should kill him, cut that fur off, and make ourselves some coats."

DAD! Really? They said that?

Shhhh. Hang on. Do you wanna hear this or not?

Jeez!

"No way! There are too many of us! Or not enough of him!"

One of the others said, "We need that salsa. We need to learn how to make ourselves strong."

A third animal said, "If he is a shaman, a true shaman, then he IS the sauce. And we need the sauce."

The pile of animals grumbled back and forth until they fell asleep. When they awoke during the night they would look across at the giant dog sleeping not far from them. They would close their eyes and dream of fur. They could run where they want, climb what they want, they might go really high in the mountains and just live there and look out across the valleys and yell to their neighbors on the opposite mountain, yes with fur they could fill the sky with their song. The cottony clouds, the chocolatey dirt, the fluffy trees, and the sweet dewy grass would all chime in. Life would be a lot better with fur.

The chihuahua shaman headed out early the next morning. The pile of animals pretended not to notice. They dozed heavy and dreamt of eating clean foods that gave them strong muscles and solid bones. They chewed as they dreamt. They salivated on one another.

Gross, dad. Then what happened?

The chihuahua shaman came back empty handed. He did make them a good little mixture of cilantro and onions but they didn't go for it. They wanted more nuts and berries. They had their own things they liked to eat, you know?

I know! Animals don't eat salsa! They eat like you said, nuts and berries and leaves and little insects.

Very true. Yes. I am glad you said that. Now, think about it for a second. If you went into the forest and dropped some salsa,

NO.

. . . or a burrito,

NO! Hahaha.

Or, OR, just think of a french fry. If you were an animal and you were going around looking for nuts and berries, but you come across this single french fry, do you think you would pass that up? You would think that thing dropped from heaven, am I right?

Hehe, I guess, but it's not good for them.

Correct! However. This chihuahua was a shaman. A very wise animal who was very powerful and if he told you his tribe knew how to make a secret food that gave strength and fur then you would believe him. And that's what they did. Because he had the power to make something they could never make on their own. Damn straight they want that! They would eat it, I'm sure! Are you going to let me tell the story or not? I have to take you to practice now so fine I will tell you the rest this evening at home. After your shower. After you shave your chest down.

So then what happened, papi?

Oh yeah where was I . . .

WAITAMINNIT a chihuahua dog is tiny! You're lying to me!

No, I have not been lying to you. This is a story because it is a story and not the news. Not history. Not true or false. A story. Now you got to sit back and listen because it's gonna knock your socks off.

My socks are off.

Because you will learn something.

I learn things every day. This is my one day to not learn!

Listen niño. You will like it!

Okay . . .

The animals woke up in early afternoon. They wiped their eyes. The chihuahua was nowhere to be found. They figured he was still out. The wind picked up. There would be a storm upon them soon, and gauging from the smell in the wind, it would carry rain. It might even carry snow. The animals did not budge from their pile. They spoke of the things they knew. They told some of the old jokes. Day turned to night and as the sun set, dreary winds arrived and the trees shrugged and leaned in strange manners. A crew of tall brooding clouds cruised low over the forest and pressed the sky down further. Rain at least was certain. They thought about how warm salsa might be.

"It probably burns your throat," someone said.

"I get indigestion easily. I hope it doesn't burn my stomach. Does it really burn?" said another.

No one knew. They thought it might taste like the bark of a certain tree. They tried to imagine the taste as the first light drops of rain fell.

The chihuahua shaman came back well after dark, well after the forest was dotted with shallow ponds, and well after the starving creatures cowered at several volleys of thunder. They were frozen in place. He brought them food. They ate what they could and climbed back on top of each other. The chihuahua looked tired. He walked over to his spot, curled up, and without saying a word, he laid his body down; it looked gaunt and shadowy in the lightning.

Lightning struck a tree near the chihuahua and the animals watched a glowing electrical blast spread across a puddle and blow up the ground beneath him. For a second he was engulfed in bright light. His body leapt into the air and fell down lifeless. Was he lifeless? If he was, then how would they get the salsa? The lightning storm smashed overhead. Layers of sheets of water in giant drops pelted the animals and they shivered together: "We don't need him to make the magical sauce. The magical sauce is inside him. It IS HIM. This chihuahua IS our sauce! Let's steal his magic!"

Their ears rang from thunder.

"Come on! We have got to make it to him! It's now or never!"

"Is it safe?"

"No! It is definitely not safe, but if we are to survive this night, we must steal his magic! It is the only way!"

"Ohhh, I don't know . . ."

And they each positioned themselves over the chihuahua.

And he kicked and groaned but they held him down. Then, each little animal stuck a nail into his skin and they laid all over his body, nursing on his blood. They suddenly fell into a deep sleep. And the creatures had variations of the same dream:

They dreamed that the sky grew heavy and pressed down upon them. Their bones ached in their sleep. They all saw a lightning bolt. They all saw a lake of pure water and they all saw the magical plant that grew the fruit that the chihuahua had been talking about. And the animals were not so fortunate. A bolt of lightning hit them. They scattered everywhere. In mid-flight and as they landed, and after they landed, they kept dreaming. The animals that had huddled in a pile now had separate dreams. Some felt their limbs lengthen. Others felt like their ears grew long and flopped by the sides of their head. There were some animals that felt their stomachs bulge and antlers sprout from their skull. The antlers were long and branchy and itchy with felt and they rolled in their sleep to get rid of the feeling. Yet others felt longer and more muscular. They dreamt of blood flowing and soft animal meat in their teeth. Certain animals dreamt of rocky hills mounting violently upward to the sky beneath the flashing storm and they grew lots of fur, yes they grew the fur, and hooves, and horns, and ears, and fangs, and some had a smooth coat of fur, and others had long shaggy coats of fur, but they knew not, for they slept and slept, as the storm raged overhead.

But not the chihuahua. He dreamt that he had fallen down a deep well that was becoming smaller at the end, but his speed of falling increased as he fell, and the walls closed in tighter and tighter around him, but they never touched him. He shut his eyes tight. He opened them. He somehow knew that he needed to get to the bottom of the well. It would be warmer there. He felt the heat radiating up. The well turned ninety degrees and became a tunnel and his falling turned into accelerated running. He ran faster and faster and kept looking for the lake of magic salsa. He could smell it somewhere out there. He could feel it. He ran faster to return to the salsa, to his family, his friends. He thought of his loved ones as salsa. The salsa was him, was inside him, was in them. He needed to return.

⁓

Eventually, the storm tired and left to wreak unruly damage somewhere else. The trees dripped. The puddles shimmered in the late morning light. The hills stood clean and proud. The chihuahua opened his eyes and couldn't believe how close the ground was. He tried to stand up, but looked down and realized he was already standing as tall as he could. The dream was somehow real! He had fallen through a tunnel and shrunk! He was excited and nervous. He looked at himself. He was short, with white hairs around his snout, his eyes bugged out, and he felt a little uneasy about everything. He felt strange about staying there to help the animals. He felt weird about leaving the shelter of the trees. He was uneasy with the idea of heading home alone. All his mastery of demeanor had somehow fled with the dream. He knew he needed to be home among his group. He headed back. The journey would take him a full year instead of five months.

Back under the sheltered canopy of trees, one animal looked at herself in a puddle and discovered she was a wolf. At first she thought she saw the chihuahua, but no, the image licked her nose at the same time she did. It moved its head from side to side when she did. Its paw met hers when she stepped into the puddle. Yes, she was a wolf. She ran back to the old place, the rock, and she discovered it was now a burnt pit with stones flung about every which way. She looked for the others but did not find them. She ran off in search of food.

Another animal awoke to discover that he was the deer with the very itchy antlers. He rubbed them on the tree trunks and bellowed to the air. His sound was still squeaky, much as it had always been. The grass in a clearing glowed with insistence and beckoned him out to it. He hopped and galloped and kicked his way there with his new long legs and he waved his antlers around like a fussy youth. That grass was so tender to nibble. But he considered a new thought: *maybe he should be careful*. Then he heard a wolf howl echo through the air. He knew he needed to stay low. This sounded like danger.

Another animal awoke to find she was a rabbit. A few of them did. They hopped out to the clearing to munch on the sparkling grass. They played in the sun. They recognized the deer from before. "Hey how did you get so big? Isn't it great to have fur? This is the best!" they asked, as they all trotted over. The deer, on seeing the grass move toward him in a solid shooting wave, somehow driven by an invisible force, fled the scene at full tilt.

The she-wolf snapped up a rabbit and tore into it. "Hey!" they yelled. The rabbits screamed and ran. The wolf gave chase. The animals could no longer understand one another. They would never again share the same old jokes. They would never enjoy sleeping in a pile or even dread sleeping in a pile. The mountain rams ran up the hills and shouted to their neighbors across the valley. They jumped off the rocks and outran the wolves. No one was speaking like they used to. The times had changed. A long winter settled in, but now the animals were ready. They knew what to do.

Hey sonny, did you like that?

Zzzzzzzzzz.

Okay . . . good night mijito querido. I love you.

Corn Woman or The Baker's Wife

A Golem is given life
with the Hebrew word EMET, which means
TRUTH, marked on its forehead.

To destroy the creature, the first letter is removed,
leaving MET, which means DEATH.

My parents moved to Venezuela from Poland. They stayed together long enough to have three children. Their first, Reynaldo, was born in 1934; the second, Alvaro, in 1937; and I, Juana Luisa Bolçek, was born in 1942, an afterthought. Well, that's what Alvaro told me when we were little. He was just kidding. I knew better. But sometimes it still hurts. I prefer to imagine that I was created under more, how shall we say, pleasant circumstances.

Anyway, between children, my father found mostly out-of-town jobs. He was a very dedicated professional. One day, he told us he was going to Panama on a temporary assignment. Sadly, it would be his last trip. He might have hit his head or something and forgotten us. Maybe he was in the hospital. We were never told. Or, maybe it is just me who was never told. Anyway, I was sure about two things: One, he never wrote to us, and two, he never returned.

I have pleasant memories of Papi before he left. One of his jobs was to survey landforms and road levels in the area. Once in a while, he'd let us go along for the ride. He would drive around, find a crack or bump or curve in the road, or whatever he was looking for, park, set up his telescope on a tripod, peer through it down the road, write on his clipboard, hang a little chain from the tripod, write down whatever that thing told him, fold it up, hand it all through the window to Alvaro, and we would be on our way again.

I could never see anything through that telescope, just my eyelashes blinking back at me. Alvaro would always take the front seat and stare in silence, hypnotizing himself with the passing landscape. He would perch sideways to face the window and focus on features of the countryside. I remember watching his eyes dart back and forth like a maniac. He looked possessed. We would often sing along with the radio. They played a lot of Mariachi music back then, as well as Tango. Carlos Gardel was everyone's favorite.

The curvy mountain roads would sometimes make me sick. Once, we had to park so I could throw up. Alvaro came over to hold my hair out of my face. Papi sat inside and tapped the steering wheel with his thumb. He seemed agitated. He looked at his watch. He squinted down the road. I was all right. I hated throwing up but it seemed to bother him more than it did me. I think Papi might have blamed himself. I climbed back in the car and went on with my singing. Alvaro hopped in, sipped his cola from a bottle, and leaned his forearm on the window, like usual. He always kept that damn window closed, even when it was really hot. I'd have to beg him to roll it down.

But, life was kind of good with father gone. There was no more yelling. The house was quiet. On weekdays, we went to an American academy to learn English. They taught elementary through high school. Reynaldo studied every night. On the weekends, Alvaro either read alone or stayed out late with his friends. Mami didn't mind. She was lenient with the boys, but preferred that I stay home. She tried to teach me needlework and cooking whenever possible, for as long as I could stand it. I had no patience for rules or measurements in my free time.

Los Campitos de Baruta was south and west of Caracas, deep in a nest of rolling hills. Today, I believe it has been absorbed by Caracas. What used to be empty woods is now quite populated. In my time, Los Campitos was built around one road with a church at the far end, up against a grove of trees. In front of the church was a large square—a plaza, where we had dances and festivals. The road was lined with shops that every little community needs: a baker, butcher, flowers, blankets, dry goods, crafts, and a repair shop. My brothers and I knew every shopkeeper. But then again, everyone knew everyone.

⌒

Over anyone else in my memory, the baker was the most remarkable figure of our town, although few people knew him well. Our little town was rife with hearsay, love, and jealousy, so it is difficult to decipher truth from fiction. Nevertheless, today, sixty years later, I still think about his story, so I am writing it down. For now it will stay in my diary, but maybe one day my children or my grandchildren will publish it. Who knows.

Anyway, Mami told me the baker was also Jewish or that he was very impressed with Jewish tradition and stories from Europe. She says he spoke intensely with Papi when we first moved there. He asked many questions about Eastern Europe and the history of our people. My guess is that Papi had little to share.

Reynaldo nicknamed our baker *Tortero* because he made the best tortillas and arepas we had ever tasted. *Toro, toro Tortilladero* Reynaldo would say, or *torrero tortero!* for short. It was a name given in admiration. The baker did not mind. He used an ancient press of solid black iron called *La Tortilladora*. The name, literally translated into English, means "the tortilla maker." But if you take the suffix, *dora* you have a common feminine first name which means *golden* or *of gold*.

The breads from that press had more of a golden taste than color, but were unmatched in neighboring towns. My brothers and I made up a story about the baker, that the press was his wife, that he made love to his wife every morning, and that their babies were the magnificent breads that kept our town fed and happy and closely knit. Tortero was single. He was in fact married to his work. It consumed him from the hours before dawn until sundown, when he would busy himself preparing dough for the following day.

Sometimes, after dark, we would see a light from the window at the back of his store. He lived behind his bakery. The building was a large, thatched bungalow with a business entrance on the street, a side door for kitchen deliveries, and a back door, which was actually the front door to his apartment. He had a study, a living room and a bedroom.

Behind the shop, there was a dirt yard with a few bushes, a large oak tree with a bench built around the trunk, and a wide grill. His screen door was usually propped open on hot evenings. Sometimes Tortero would sip beer and smoke stinky tobacco with the shoe repair man. They would mumble and laugh together. They were funny to watch, like two fuzzy old dogs.

It was okay for us kids to be playing in his yard, and sometimes he would play kickball with us, but we'd inevitably get yelled at because there were too many things in the way, like his grill or the trees or the bushes. Or his window.

Yes, I cracked his window. Once. I cried and ran in and said I was sorry. He offered me a *pan dulce de guayaba* but I never liked them much. Not enough sugar and too much dough. I said, "No thank you," and that I would pay for the window out of my own pocket.

I didn't get into as much trouble as I thought. My brothers fixed it for me. We found a cheap window in Caracas that Mami paid for. Reynaldo and Alvaro finished the work in about an hour. I was very grateful.

⌒

One summer evening we were playing hide-and-go-seek in the church plaza. I looked under a wagon but found someone there. Someone else was in a little planter box I liked. I tried the barrel in front of the flower shop but couldn't keep out of sight. I checked behind the flower shop . . . and then I saw the bench under Tortero's tree. No one would ever find me there. I crawled under it and waited for twenty minutes. It was maybe the greatest hiding place ever but also extremely boring. No one ever did find me. I got up to sneak back to the plaza to win the final round.

I heard Alvaro calling me home, but I didn't want him to find me before I could tag the plaza. I passed by Tortero's side door when the odd color of light caught my eye. It was a sleepy dull yellow, lit by a couple lanterns, one on the wall and one on his desk. A breeze touched my face and high above the branches of the great oak tree, a black cloud took shape in the evening sky. He had left his side door open to let the breeze flow through the kitchen. I could smell the heat of his ovens. I thought, *what if I just poked my head in, to see if he would notice me.*

It seemed like nobody was home. I slipped quietly through the doorway. I was grinning. I thought it would be funny to yell *boo!* and startle him at his desk. But he wasn't there. Where was Tortero? Maybe he had seen me first and was going to sneak up on me while I was sneaking up on him! Alvaro called me again from the plaza. Oh! What was this? I found him asleep on his couch. Then I noticed his leg sticking out from under a blanket. His foot was bare and smooth, like a woman's.

It was a woman's leg. She looked dead! She lay there absolutely still. Her face was covered, and her leg, from below the knee, was sticking out in the air over the arm of the couch. I backed quietly out of the study, slunk back through the kitchen, ran out into the night, and ran right up into Alvaro's arms. It was late by then and the other children had gone home. "What is the matter with you?" he said.

"I think Tortero has found a wife. But she's dead."

Alvaro told me that I was silly and we would go over and check on the baker. He was certain it was Tortero lying on the couch. He took me by the hand. No one had ever seen the baker with a woman friend. But then, he knew every woman in town, so why not? Why wouldn't one of them come over, maybe have some tea, and then fall asleep on his couch? Maybe he was in the bathroom or went to the bedroom closet for a sweater or something.

We didn't want to bother the baker with nosy questions, so we snuck up to the window. Alvaro held me out of the way and pressed his face up to the glass. He saw the baker. He was reading a large book at his desk and then periodically standing and moving his lips and bobbing his head forward in a rhythmic fashion, like men do in temple. He wore a skullcap, a kippah.

Alvaro stood back from the window. He let me peer in. I stood on a box. He pointed, whispering "See, there's the baker right there.

He's fine." He took me by the arm away from the window.

"Hey!" I said. I grabbed the windowsill to hang on but it was crusty and old. Part of it fell off in my hands.

On hearing the noise, the baker, normally a mild-tempered man, dropped what he was doing and flew to the window, yelling. He tore off his prayer shawl, held it in his fist, and shook it at us. He yelled at us to get away, *Get out! Get out!* But we were *out*. We ran away and went home.

No one told Mami what happened that night. But, boy, was she curious. We couldn't tell her, and maybe she didn't really want to know, because it would force her to do her job as a mother: to prevent us from doing anything interesting. We did tell Reynaldo. With Reynaldo, we made plans to find out exactly what the baker was up to.

A late night of stealth and sneaking was going to be most amusing. We had no plans to expose the baker or to accuse him of any wrongdoing. We felt it was too far out of his character to have actually killed anyone. Or was it? The idea of a midnight spy mission was certainly very amusing. We already knew he had a dead woman on his couch. Who knew what else we would discover!

As part of the arrangement I would put on my pajamas and go to bed as usual. No one told Mami. I kissed her goodnight and set some clothes next to my bed after she turned out the lights. Alvaro would come and wake me up to leave. I was so excited that I found it hard to sleep. I kept tossing and turning, dreaming of the baker's crazy face stretching out in an elongated scream from inside a glass cage.

⌐

But what I wanted to happen wasn't what my brothers wanted to happen. Alvaro and Reynaldo woke me up the next morning. "What! Why didn't you . . .?" I said, rising and rubbing my eyes.

"Shhht!" said Reynaldo and covered my mouth. "You're too little."

"What do you mean? I'm nine years old! I'm big now."

"You're too young to come out with us so late at night. We just checked on a few things and didn't stay long. You would have made too big a deal of it."

"Okay . . ." I was frustrated. "So tell me. What did you find?" I said, folding my arms and sitting up in bed.

"Nothing but an old witch woman . . . who says she's coming to get you!" He said, tickling me.

"Stop it!" I said, trying to push him away. "You cut it out right now and tell me what you saw!"

"What's all the noise about?!" Mami yelled.

"Shhht!" Said Reynaldo. "You're getting Mama in on this! Nothing Ma– we'll help with breakfast right away!"

Alvaro sat on the bed next to me. "Okay I'll tell you. It's just this—yes. Tortero does seem to have a woman sleeping on the couch. He stays up very late studying from a big old book and praying." He and Reynaldo looked at one another. "We think she's sick, because he stands over the couch and prays and then goes back to the table. We were there pretty late. He was still up. She's covered with that blanket head to toe now and she doesn't move. She's probably really sick."

But who she was, nobody knew. Then suddenly one day she appeared. She was selling bread at the counter while Tortero worked the ovens. This was to be the new way. It was good for him too. He seemed happy. He took more time off and sat out back, watching his tree, smoking tobacco, chatting with people. He played kickball with us.

Who's the woman? people would ask. *A cousin*, he would say, the daughter of his uncle's wife from Tierra Linda, to stay with him and help with the bakery. *Ah, well then!* they would say. You'd have to ask the baker because she was such a quiet woman. She didn't need to talk much. She only responded to business questions like, *When will you have this or that kind of bread?* or *How much is so and so?*

She was pretty, perhaps beautiful, but quiet and downward-looking. She had dark skin and rich, unruly black hair. Also, she had a few very thick hairs growing between her eyebrows. They were not easy to miss, as her eyes were black and dramatic, edged with thick lashes and topped by those eyebrows, which looked like two black caterpillars with slender tails, ready to joust one another.

We liked her. We really did. People began to wonder if Tortero wasn't perhaps having relations with her. Why not? She was pretty, helpful, and within a few weeks she was starting to show. Did she arrive pregnant? Maybe that's why he brought her to Los Campitos, because her boyfriend in Tierra Linda left her pregnant and she wanted to have a new life here. Well, no problem. We understood.

I heard that people saw them sitting close at church, letting their thighs touch. I believe what they say because I saw the pair lightly touching fingers, as if they couldn't help it, while walking through the marketplace. She was looking radiant in a white cotton dress with her shoulders uncovered, and her belly was getting huge.

Soon it became clear that they were probably lovers. The touching, the glances, and the hand holding increased. The town was quiet in their presence, but rumors abounded. Why would he have a child with his cousin? Is she his cousin? She's not his cousin, they would say. She's a prostitute he brought in from another town who wanted to reform and start a new life. Every theory they'd make up was outlandish or plain ridiculous. They would make up anything to satisfy their cravings for information.

So what, I thought, if they have a child. Who cares if it's his or not. He loves her and he's kind to her. That's all any family could hope for. I hoped that God would bless me with a man so gentle and caring. That was how I felt.

Once, about a year later, some children playing kickball under the huge oak tree lost control of the ball and it happened to hit Tortero's woman in the back of the head. It was embarrassing to watch. She had been looking even more beautiful and elegant lately, after the birth of the child. Her hair had grown smooth and long. The child was plump and precious and somewhat freckled. They lavished the little boy with love and called him *Pinto*. His real name was Pedro.

But when the ball hit her on the head, it seemed to touch something deep within her that we nor she had ever seen before. Who knows what was behind it, but she turned slowly and, without actual anger, she stated plainly, *It would be safer for you to play in the plaza.* Her calm attitude had a chilling effect.

The kids were shocked because they'd never heard her give a direct order. She'd been such a shy and quiet person. Then the moment got worse. In the silence, as we were gawking, someone said, *You had a child by your cousin!*

And the lid was off from that moment on. *Baker's got a girlfriend!* She went inside. Other comments were made, but Tortero and some shop owners chased the kids out and told them play in the plaza. The kids were no longer interested in their game. They scattered home, grunting and kicking up dirt as they shuffled in different directions. I thought the kids were nasty to taunt her like that. She hadn't been so mean. She had put her foot down and they couldn't handle it.

Anyway, they were just looking for a reason to repeat all the fiction the town had been dreaming up. Most of the kids' mothers brought them in by the ear to apologize at the bakery counter. Some did not, because they believed the hearsay.

⁓

Despite all the buzz about the woman and Tortero, it was never confirmed whether they were an item or not. In fact, it turned out that young men cultivated fantasies about her and overtly sought her attention, despite her obvious closeness to the baker. She would smile and chat at the counter but never gave anybody any *ideas*.

And that's how things got a little bumpy on the night of the Festival of Lights. This is a celebration where our town dolls itself up with lanterns and streamers that crisscross the plaza in bright colors. Everyone participates. Musicians set up and play in the square. It is traditionally a time when young men ask out the young women they care for.

Well, nobody asked me out. But Mami and I strolled down to see how it all looked. There were people in small groups wandering with bottles of booze, locked arm over shoulder, some young couples, and groups of young guys laughing and yelling down the street. We passed girls practicing the steps to a dance they all knew ... I didn't know it. I was clumsy, but I didn't care. If I wanted to have fun, I just danced around like a freak and cranked my arms and waggled my knees a lot. Everybody would laugh and sometimes join in. That was okay with me.

Then, we heard screams. People rushed to the grove of trees behind the church. Apparently, one of the young bucks had made advances on the baker's woman. Then, after refusal, he and his soccer gang had closed in and chased her into the woods. She was surrounded.

She was immensely strong. In her efforts to escape, she broke one of the young men's arms. It was his screams we heard. She fled further into the wilderness outside our town. The young men went home. Tortero took some friends and went looking for her. They found her walking alone, at the top of a steep hill, wringing her hands. She was unresponsive to their calls. Who knows what those guys had done.

Tortero walked gently over. She never made eye contact.

He reached out. Once he was close enough, she threw him right down the hill. Instead of trying again, he just picked himself up, brushed himself off, and went home. He looked bruised and worried.

~

The following truth replaced rumors for the next week: She was out there, wandering the hills, so agitated that she couldn't come down, and Tortero had let her alone to wander.

But what could he do? Chase her, tie her up, throw her over a horse, and force her to stay home on the couch until she got over it? Or is that how it all started. . . ? I wondered. We all wondered.

Soon came reports that she was sneaking through the town late at night, growling in the alleys and scratching at people's windows. I'm glad I never heard that first hand. I'd be really scared. They said her hair was thicker and more tangled than ever. Her skin was dirty and smudged and she slunk around town completely naked, like an animal. She would beat up drunk men late at night as they stumbled home. I thought it was funny, because now families knew when a man had been out getting drunk—he'd show up at breakfast with a black eye or welts on his face. *Oh, so the bruja got you*, they would say. *That'll teach you to drink!* Well, bully for her, I thought. Now we've got a superhero.

But the children were afraid. Including her own child. Flower pots were tossed, windows were broken, and other random malevolent acts occurred every night. No one actually saw her do it, but there was no end to the *I-came-face-to-face-with-a-naked-savage-woman!* tales.

Little Pinto got more and more cranky and wouldn't sleep at night. Tortero had to constantly care for the baby and it was really tough on him. An older girl, Lupita, came forward to help the poor man. Things went better, but the baker's cousin never came back down from the hills.

Months later, she was spotted soaking her feet in a mud puddle, back propped against a tree, having animated conversations with a stray dog sleeping next to her. She was muddy, with bloody scratches, and still noble. She'd covered herself with a ragged *ruana*.

When the neighbors brought Tortero to talk with her, she erupted in laughter.

She told them many exposing things about the baker. She insulted him directly and pointed at him with a long and crooked fingernail. He was silent and lowered his head. The others didn't know whether they should be looking at him or her or the dog. It was embarrassing for everyone. She spat her words out through teeth that had rotted or broken off.

She was a scary sight to behold. Tortero tried to reason with her but she threw mud at him and yelled, "I hate you! I wish I'd never been born! I can't stand what you did to me, you desperate son of a bitch pig!"

No one understood what she meant by that. Could it have been the pregnancy? But the way she delivered it was clear enough. They stood back to let Tortero calm her down gently, in whatever manner possible, to try to communicate in their own intimate language. However, something he said definitely did not work. She lunged at him. The two started wrestling frantically in the mud. She soon had him pinned and was choking the life out of him. The neighbors ran to peel her off.

And as they pulled her away, she dropped to her knees in front of Tortero, sobbing heavily. When they let go, she grabbed for his legs, not to knock him down, but instead to hug him as if she was a little girl. "Honey, I'm sorry . . ." she said. "Please let me die. I wanna die now." The baker cried and pet her hair, which had so much dirt and leaves in it, it looked like the hide of an animal. He looked over at the tiny crowd who had come to help.

They stared back at him, unnerved by the woman and her repeated requests to die. He asked them to please go away so the two could be alone. They did. They had no idea how he was going to get through this, but he seemed quite resolved. *Of course he's not going to kill her, don't be silly*, someone said. They were boiling with curiosity. So the little crowd walked behind some trees to hide.

They stayed far enough out of sight but not too far to prevent them from keeping an eye on Tortero and his wife. Here's what they saw: She knelt down in front of him, crying into his kneecaps. Her arms were wrapped around his legs. He stooped over her, stroking her hair, again and again. He backed away and she lost balance, but he helped her stay upright. Then he took to his knees in front of her, so they were on the same level.

They hugged one another gently for a long while. They did not say a word or even utter a sound. Then, he held her face in his hands and kissed her on the mouth. He kept holding her face and she looked up at him, a little cross-eyed, both sad and happy. Then, with his thumb, he rubbed the area where her eyebrows grew together. Her eyes rolled up in her head as she closed them. She looked very relaxed. He wiped again, and with a frown, she slipped from his arms, as if she had fainted from exhaustion.

The *ruana* became the biggest thing between the two of them. Soon it covered her completely. Fallen leaves from the tree mounded up against her, hiding her entirely from sight. Then she was gone. Did she get and up go somewhere? They lost track of her through the trees. *What happened? Is she gone?* They came to the baker and asked, finding nothing but leaves where she had been sitting.

Is she . . . dead? said someone else.

The baker was scooping a large pile of corn flour into the old blanket. "She is gone." He smiled. His face was wet from tears.

At the same time, Pinto, who had been sleeping at the bakery, also disappeared. Lupita was beside herself with worry. Tortero was still out in the hills with the others. She'd gone to the back room to check on the baby only to find his crib a complete mess. She said it looked like he had crawled into a pile of masa, ate some, and threw it up in his crib.

It was slopped all over the little bed, but nowhere else. Pinto was nowhere to be found. Lupita looked for the child everywhere. She went to every house she could think of. She came by our place but we had only ever seen the boy on a couple of occasions, much less take him into our home without them knowing about it.

When Tortero and the others came down from the hills, Lupita was distraught. But he didn't seem too concerned. He hugged her and held her hand and said that the child was now with his mother and wouldn't be coming back. I wonder if that made her stop worrying.

On the following Monday, the breads were sweeter than usual. The town remarked how delicious they were. The arepas he made on that day were truly of a light and crispy texture and a flavor that I have never tasted before or since. Mami brought some home, wrapped up in towels, and handed me one. It was still hot from his oven. She had an excited look on her face. "You'll never believe what happened! The baker has announced his intention to marry the baby's caretaker! He has made special arepas and is giving them to anyone who comes to his shop!"

What was in those arepas, I wondered. Hope. Heartbreak. A baker's tears.

⁓

Three months later, he married Lupita at the church. Everyone showed up. Everyone in five towns showed up. It was incredible. Anyone who had ever tasted his bread or knew about his baking showed up.

His odd history and misfortunes always went with the notoriety of his breads. Anyone who heard the tales that stretched from him in every direction, came to wish him luck for the future.

They were happy for the next year. Then she miscarried. Poor Tortero was gloomy. He would stamp around the shop and get impatient with the customers. He'd yell at the kids. No one played in his yard anymore so he'd go over to the plaza to yell at them. He'd even go out to the soccer fields to yell at them. The kids left him alone. My brothers were gone to school in the United States by that time. It was just Mami and me living in a little house with Alvaro's empty chicken coop behind it.

Tortero and Lupita left town. She was seen a couple times in the market but no one knew where they were staying. They had disappeared long enough for us to find good bread for everyone, but of course we had to buy it in Caracas.

They took turns driving twice a week and set up a table in the plaza to hand out the bread. Mami and I couldn't drive so we would ride along with our neighbors and help lug the loaves around in big baskets. The smell of fresh bread eased my carsickness a great deal, by the way.

One day, it was the shoe repairman's turn to drive. He had gone with the flower lady and her family. They gained a juicy tidbit of information on the way home. "You'll never guess who's coming back!" They said. "Yes. The baker! And they have a newborn with them. Did they adopt? No, he insists it is his own. Yes, we saw them. They were walking by the roadside. They expect to return in a few weeks. They send you all their best and can't wait to see you."

Then we should have a welcome party! Despite his antisocial habits, most people understood and wanted their nutty old Tortero back. We all missed his bread. Yes, there would be a very warm welcome home party for him and his beautiful young bride and their newborn.

The ladies couldn't wait to meet the baby. I admit I was curious too. Just to see how the little guy resembled his Papa with a newborn tadpole face. I was there when the baker opened up his bungalow and invited people in to meet the newborn. They were hushed and giggling. Two women prodded and primped the baby's little lair, the same one Pinto used, and tended to his collar. I admit this one did look more like Tortero and even had something of his mother in him, but it was hard to ignore the fact that he had four distinct marks between his eyebrows. They were barely darker than his skin, almost like freckles.

One of the women licked her thumb to wipe them, thinking it was dirt. "Hey! Don't do that! I'll get that!" he snapped. Tortero's eyes bulged out of his head. He had been gabbing and crowing across the room.

"She was just helping," they told him.

"I've got this...you don't need to help. But thank you!" He grinned nervously. His hand was shaky. He smiled and gestured at the table. He looked around at everyone. "Don't worry about a thing, just eat some cake and enjoy yourselves. We will take good care of the baby. Thank you...thank you all!"

WHEN THE PHONE RANG

In the years between the wars, there was a prisoner. He had been plucked from the streets of his town because he was walking home with bread on the wrong day. Because the black smoke blew south rather than north. Because invading forces mistook themselves for rebel forces. Because rebel forces mistook themselves for allied forces. Because the crusaders were in fact supporters. Because a gunnery sergeant spoke like Yosemite Sam.

Because that sergeant howled and gesticulated from his perch, farting out last night's Spam chili in the back of a truck picking off *Hajis* and then he shot a little boy, after the boy had shooed his sister home on her bicycle. The *because* didn't matter anymore. This prisoner had been detained in the same manner as any other enemy combatant, if they are not killed on sight.

It was well within the broad and permissive guidelines defining enemy combatants, as they are wont to flex and shake like the disco shorts of a midnight cowboy, snapping her gum and smiling on the cellphone behind the bushes, under the stairwell of military protocol, commingling with bloodlust and prescription-addled shell shock.

The prisoner was named Muhammad. Muhammad had been chained to a concrete floor in a stress position for four days. This was the fifteenth such session in his broad career as a prisoner for the past four years. His knees felt like railroad pikes had been sledgehammered down through the marrow. His eyes felt like they wept blood, and his teeth were folding in on themselves, or maybe the entire thing was an illusion, but the feelings were convincing enough to make him believe that he would never die but that he would in fact see heaven unfold before him right there in his cell, shitting himself, chained to the floor, viewing it glow through his hood, to the tune of the music played through the speakers above. Inside that selfsame hood, he had carefully traced out the lines of tree-filled windows with his mind's eye.

His windows were dressed with blowing curtains and mounted in walls of flowery wallpaper. The ringing in his ears was birds chirping by day and crickets by night. He tapped his thighs in remembrance to the drum beats of his youth, now burned and stamped out like rank cigarettes made of chewing gum paper, stuffed with camel dung.

Muhammad hated the invaders. He prayed for vengeance. He felt himself slowly dying in his cell. He called out in his brain to Allah to come visit and take him away. His mouth was no longer operating efficiently. He muttered and sobbed. He had no further hope of returning home. His new home was dark, but well lit within the universe he had created. His couch was soft. Thick with rugs. His record player worked. His television was boring. Delightfully boring and irrelevant. He sat against the couch on the floor and gazed for hours at the shifting images on his black and white television set. Egyptian movies from the 1950s and 60s streamed endlessly. Oum Kheltoum sang to full auditoriums with her arms out wide, sound emanating from her chest, the core of her love, as he dozed lightly, deep in the summery afternoons of the galaxy behind his black hood.

Corporeal pain was the last thing to tie Muhammad to this world. It confined him like a shipyard rope, tight against his midriff, squeezing out the final drops of his humanity. His tears would not spill forth. His eyes dripped something slowly, more viscous than tears, which he assumed was blood. The muscles in his face were also cramped and bleeding, for they were just as locked into position as the rest of his body. The guards did not let him stand nor sleep, but he was removed from his cage daily for prayers and questioning. He had no ideas. He had no opinions. He knew a few people. Those people were doing their business. He did not want their business. He did want the guards dead and everything around him destroyed.

Muhammad lived his dwindling and meager life completely within the flowing drapes he had traced inside his hood. The hood was locked around his neck. His hands were chained to another chain that fixed his ankles to the floor, thus forcing him to crouch, forever. He kept his eyes on his windows. He watched the trees move beyond them. He saw birds and clouds passing. He had a prayer rug rolled up against the eastern wall. He turned on the television. Then the phone rang. He let it ring. *This phone doesn't ring*, he thought. *How can it?* The phone stopped ringing. He watched the undulating shapes of black and grey move in and out among the various dramas broadcast on his modest television. Late afternoon soon arrived. It was the hour of his nap. The phone rang. He picked it up. He heard a tone. "*bip bip boop bip boop boop boop*" Couldn't be. It sounded like Morse code. He hung up the phone.

He remembered Morse code. He had studied it in school. It was a fascination for him for a while, a compulsion where, as he listened to his favorite music, he would try to match the lyrics spelled out in Morse code to the rhythm of the song, by clacking his teeth softly inside his closed mouth which worked rarely, except for the occasional American delta blues, to interesting effect. The message on the telephone must be expressly for him. But who would call him on his imaginary phone? It must be god. He should answer the phone and listen to the message of god, surely this was some kind of divine intervention. Maybe god was finally going to visit and thought he would be considerate enough to call first to clarify matters, perhaps there are conditions that he should know about. Any good scholar knows that god has plenty of conditions for pilgrims on their way to heaven.

Muhammad thanked his lucky stars and thought about the phone call for three days. He changed the position of the phone also. It had been on a table by the television but instead, he moved it closer to the couch where he spent most of his time, so he could talk on the phone and gaze dreamily out the windows, or maybe talk about the programs he would be watching on the television. Yes, the phone would be closer so he could answer it quickly, perhaps by the first ring. Perhaps as the phone first sets to ring, like this: rrrrhello! Yes, this is Muhammad! God? I have been waiting for so long to hear from you. Yes, I would be so overwhelmed with joy to live with you in your kingdom. Yes, I have kept to the five pillars. No, no cheating or lying. I am good to my fellow men. And women! I am kind to my mother! No, no masturbation. No. I am so sorry. That time was an accident. Thank you for understanding, god. God you are merciful! God you are great!

The days spun on. The glee resulting from the prospect of receiving a telephone call from god built a tiny cabin in his soul, raising a puff of smoke from its chimney that made it easier for Muhammad to form words when he was brought in for questioning. Everything was better. The air within his sanctuary with the flowing curtains was always fresh and filled with light. The birds chirped calmly. The couch rose up to his ear for sweet dozing. His prayer rug was right where it had always been. His rug had a compass at the top.

Here, in this world traced inside his hood, the compass sometimes would spin for a few minutes. He would stare at it and try to feel the magnetic poles blowing past him like storm clouds, or maybe it was Mecca on a train car, or better yet, maybe the compass was stuck to the Kaaba which had escaped on a flying carpet to avoid the fundamentalists of the world, turning the compass round and around. The phone rang again, once. He couldn't reach it in time. He picked it up anyway. Hello? No. He did hear a dial tone. He liked the sound of the dial tone. He listened until it stopped. Then he listened to the silence.

Muhammad pressed his finger on the button in the cradle of the telephone and it began to ring. He lifted his finger immediately.

Rrrrrrhello!

Bip bip boop bip boop boop boop

Sorry?

Boop boop bip bip boop.

Then nothing. He hung up. He thought about the combination of short and long pulses for the rest of the day. *Bip bip boop bip boop boop boop* continued by *boop boop bip bip boop*. So odd. He thought to himself in Morse code. He spelled out every thought, every concept, everything that entered his mind for that afternoon in morse code. It took him the entire following day to correctly spell his thoughts on the matter. He gazed at himself in the bathroom mirror. He bowed and rinsed his face. *Boop boop bip bip boop*, he thought. Then, the inkling of an understanding edged in upon him. No. Couldn't be! How silly. This is how god chooses to communicate? Muhammad laughed to himself and rinsed his face again. He walked back to the couch and grabbed a pen and some paper. He wrote the following,

Kif 7alik shu 3am ta3mil (Howzzit goin wussup).

Allah speaks Arabish text slang crap? How could this be? Muhammad was on high alert. He couldn't believe it. Had he heard the code correctly? He was determined to find out. He placed the pad and pen next to the phone. The guards picked him up for questioning. He wouldn't speak. They soaked him in his hood. He imagined rain pouring down his windows. He gasped and gurgled. He couldn't believe what he had written. Could god be playing a trick on him? Perhaps this is a part of his torture. Somehow, the guards had found a way to enter his sanctuary. Muhammad wished for death. He no longer wished to be visited by god. The last thing he needed was to be visited by an asshole prison guard dressed up like god, if that could possibly be done, but if they were faking god then why not fake godly speaking? Why would Allah, praised be his name, choose to communicate with him in that Arabish text slang crap?

Muhammad sat and watched the television dozing mindlessly for a good long time. He practiced breathing slowly, so slowly, almost not breathing at all. He held tight to his jumpsuit. He felt the fabric against his skin. He became aware of the sandals wrapping his feet. He felt his breath entering the duct in his hood. He closed his eyes almost all the way. The curtains moved by the windows. Then, all of a sudden, he noticed a face slowly rising outside the near window. It had a mostly bald forehead with one long wisp of hair, moving with the breeze. It was the head of a man. The man had been seriously charred on the head. He was not balding, this was all that was left. Parts of his skull shone through his skin. One eye was missing. Most of his nose was missing. The man smiled, but then, half of his face was gone. His teeth were exposed. He couldn't help but smile. Muhammad's heart leapt out of his shirt. He felt his hood fly off his head. He lost track of his breathing. The hood hadn't actually gone anywhere, so Muhammad began to suffocate. He forced the words *What the devil!*

No. Not the devil, said the stranger, and he went away.

This couldn't have been a trick. The guards did not have the wherewithal to enter his mind in such a manner. Really, it was obviously some sort of trick, but nothing like he had ever experienced before, in his exhaustive prison career. Could there have been a drug in the water they used on him the other day? Was that yesterday or two days ago, he couldn't remember. Maybe it was three days ago. Muhammad shook his head a few times. He tried to become present in his prison cell. He tried to remember what his cage felt like, what it smelled like. It became difficult to remember. Inside his sanctuary, he took the stress position of his physical body. It was very painful. He couldn't manage it for longer than five minutes. He had to rest. There was no way to sleep it off. The man in the window stated clearly that he was not the devil. But the devil is known to lie.

Then, the phone rang. Muhammad did not want to pick it up. It rang for five minutes. Then it rang again for an hour. Then the phone rang for the rest of the day. Muhammad's brain, his sweet and soft brain that had held up so well for four years of punishment, was now finding that its supporting timbers were no more than wet rags at the core. The entire structure of his elaborate, life-giving scaffolding began to rot into a stew; a tagine made of rifle butts and missile tips, bullet holes and jail bars, a concoction soaked with anger, resentment, and hatred. At last, he answered the phone.

Hello?

Bip bip boop bip boop boop boop.

Noooo . . . no no no no no no no!

Muhammad heard light breathing. He was very quiet. He pressed the receiver more tightly against his head, pouring his ear down into the wires that might lead him out of prison, somewhere, somehow.

The voice took another breath. *You chased me away.*

Muhammad was stunned. He had no idea how to respond. He said,

I did not chase you away!

You called me the devil. You looked at me like I am some kind of madman. Who do you think you are, anyway?

You are not the devil?

No.

Aaaallah?

Muhammad's eyebrows raised up to his forehead and his forehead raised all the way back to his ears. He crammed the phone further against his ear, listening to the line so carefully, it was as if he could now hear the distant chatter of all telephone telemetry across the circuits for thousands of miles.

Certainly not.

Question marks bounded out of Muhammad's skull in every which way. He was now so afraid and yet so fascinated that it tripped his psychological governor and he lost consciousness altogether.

The guards found him shortly thereafter and doused him with water. They allowed him to sit on the floor with his pants on. They brought him some hummus. He felt much more comfortable. They brought him some water. He sat in silence. The guards lowered the volume of the music. It played less often. Muhammad had the chance to think it all through a little better. Chased him away? He had done no such thing. Who was that, why wouldn't he knock? Why was his head so badly scalded? Did he need medical attention? Does he need a place to sleep? But just a second here, this was Muhammad's sanctuary, inside his head, and now there was a visitor, not just a visitor, but a peeping tom, a half-exploded peeping tom and maybe even an enemy spy.

An enemy spy? Muhammad had no enemies. No political enemies anyway. He sold shoes and used watches at the *souk* on weekends, before he was detained. That old bastard Ali down at the end of the lane was quite the boorish ass however, but bless his soul, he might have made it out of town or was probably dead, hamdoullah, by the grace of god, but not this god. This was no god. This was a character who seemed to want to talk, despite his grisly appearance. Muhammad sat on the couch and alternated his attention between his television and the breeze playing in the curtains. He fell deeply asleep.

He was awakened by the telephone. He felt the first ring internally, deep in his core like a gurgling. The second ring began by shaking itself free of his innards, then it bubbled through his veins. The third ring jangled his very skeleton. Every iteration of the sound wave poured into his bones and from there, vibrated the cells of his body. The bell was as nerve-wracking as a fire alarm, but here there was no exit available. The emergency was all time, every day, every hour. No use for an alarm. He answered the phone on the fourth ring.

Yes.

Yes.

Do not play games with me, please.

This is no game.

Please tell me what you want from me. I have told the guards all that I know. Are you working for them?

By no means am I working for them.

What can I do for you, in the name of Allah, blessed be his name?

I am here to help.

Who are you? An angel? Are you Gabreel?

I am many things. I am a prisoner, like you. I was in Auschwitz. I was in the reeducation camps of Vietnam, of China. I have been in the places that have terror scarred into their name. Dubrava. Abu Ghraib. Guantanamo.

How?

I am you. I am your pain. I am The Pain. You may call me Abdelaziz.

How did you manage to get locked up in so many prisons?

Think about it some more.

I don't know what to think.

The phone went silent.

Hello?

Muhammad had no idea what all this meant. If he had been fed a hallucinogen four or five days ago, it surely would have left his system by now. Nothing else mattered. He had to know more. Who was this voice? How could he possibly speak without half a face? But of course this is a concoction of his own making. He had lined the inside of his hood with windows and curtains of his design. The phone was his. Of course. He had made it. Muhammad had invented his world, he lived in it, he found sanctuary there, and now there was an invader! With a story to tell, perhaps? Perhaps he could answer questions. Muhammad was too tired to ask any questions and the soldiers had already asked him all the questions he could possibly answer. He was an empty husk.

A few days later, the telephone rang. Muhammad was ready. He was also a bit more relaxed and prepared.

Hey-lo.

Yes.

Yes what?

Today I have called to tell you that these guards are not the enemy.

Oh.

Yes. You are to hold them in your heart from now on as if they were your brothers.

No.

Yes.

Who is this?

Abdelaziz. I have told you my name.

Are you a soldier? Are you with them? Are you the commanding officer?

Not at all. I am here with you.

So the soldiers are my brothers, their rifles scratch my back, and the bombs, they are my toys?

Ha-ha.

Ha-ha? Just what do you mean by ha-ha? Can you get me out of here?

Maybe. We might have to wait a bit longer.

Wait for what? Wait for them to run out of ammunition? Wait for them to run out of their despicable manners? Wait for them to run out of the will to control me?

Please relax.

Why should I relax when my life is spiraling down the drain? When it is a risk to my life to walk home with bread while being Arabic? Why should I relax when it is forbidden to go here or there while being from somewhere else? Why must I live my life out in this cage because of racial profiling, because of someone else's paranoid determination?

They act like that because they are scared. They are terrified.

Oh yes of course. Because I said BOO and they are all now afraid. This is the most terrifying sound I can make; BOOOOOOO!!!!

This is the sound of two cultures interfacing. When commerce is no longer sufficient, battles ensue. The cultures collide. Your conservatives versus their conservatives. Trust me. They are compassionate people. They are fascinated by the sound of your language and are also disgusted by it. They fear the sound of your vowels. Your 'ayin. Your qoph. They know it is beautiful and yet still they hate it. They find it repulsive. They find your culture revolting yet fascinating. They think about you often. How can you allow your women to dress like that? How can you run your business like that? How can you waste your natural resources like that? It is strange to them and yet, they want to own it. They want to do your things for you, to correct your wrongs. In the same way, your culture finds their culture atrocious and invasive.

Their culture is strange to you and your people. You wish they would stop. You think they are silly. You like their food. They think your food is weird. You want to be in Hollywood with their women. With their women's breasts. With their g-strings and their pasties. With their soft white children, swimming in their pools.

Muhammad could not believe what he was hearing. He loved the sound of his own language.

Their language is void of all meaning! It sounds like someone is kicking the stomach of a dying pig in heat! Ours is the language of god! Our writing is holy! Our calligraphy! They have nothing like that! And why in the name of god did you choose to contact me in Arabish? That mongrel savage language!

You used to speak it quite often.

What! Me? No!

To that woman in the birkha with her breasts out. You would ogle. She would chat with you and take your money.

Oh! No, I just happened to find her website. My friend showed me one day. Anyway I stopped that! Never mind that! She was evil!

Arabish is the perfect language for you. It represents your base desires, everything that you hate yet still fascinates you. This is the source of hatred. Fixation. Kissing cousins. Objectification, power, resistance. So fragile, so close, so disgusted by one another, and yet so attracted.

She was a wretched bitch! She took my money for nothing! She was probably in league with the conservative assholes to make a mockery of people like me, the average ones, the moderates! We are ready to live in a modern world! Stuck in the middle of politics and war! Victimized by every side!

Enough insults. They believe they are protecting the world.

From what? For whom? Okay, tell me what does it mean when they kill our children and bomb a hospital?

Why did the chicken cross the road?

Is that supposed to be funny?

Think about it. What does it mean?

What does what mean?

They bomb because it is in their nature. There is no answer. There are a million answers.

Oh, then there should be an all out condemnation of Israelis, Jews, Arabs, Palestinians, Greeks, Turks, Russians, every single better-than-thou American . . . who am I leaving out? They all throw bombs!

And they all receive bombs. Why don't you tell me: what does it say about their nature when they kill children and bomb a hospital?

Because if it is in their nature then it is not about options or politics, it is about their evil nature.

Bombs are built to kill humans. Bombs have one single function.

Bombs don't kill people. People do.

Bombs are just bombs. But more important, why do people keep building bombs and launching them at other people? Think about why they do it. Please.

I am not talking about people, I am talking about nations! I am not being metaphysical. I am not playing your game.

Neither am I. Bombs are built to kill and destroy. End of story.

So you are saying they are killers. That it is in their nature to be killers.

As are you.

I am not talking about our nation.

Not all of their nation are killers. And not all of your nation are killers.

I am talking about the children in the playground and at the hospital. They die playing on the beach. They die by the side of the road.

I am specifically talking about the warmongers. People are perversely fascinated by charnel. These nations did not take a consensus or vote together to determine where the next bomb would land. There is one man who made that choice.

Oh, I thought they were a democracy.

War is never a democracy. Peace is perhaps a democracy. At least it feigns democracy. War, a totalitarianism, is sold to a democracy as a temporary "minimal risk/maximum profit" endeavor. The heads of nations convince their public that the bomb attacks are guaranteed to be clean strikes. Backed by cold science. They call their bomb strikes surgical. Don't you get it? Surgical. That's why they aim at hospitals.

Now that was a joke.

Busted.

And what of the burned baby held by a crying man in a crowded funeral procession? How am I supposed to process this?

If you process it you are involved in the war.

It is unavoidable, the violence is everywhere. In the streets. Film. Photographs. Right before my eyes! So what should I do, slash my wrists?

If you slash your wrists you are participating in the exchange of violence.

I don't understand that. My life doesn't belong to you or anyone else. I don't agree with that assessment at all.

We are locked in a crisis of revenge. Cause and effect.

Okay, well then I guess I can go shopping now.

Rather than react violently to the violent emotional exchange, we must accept and say the violence stops with me, rather than the violence begins with me, or the violence will be continued by me.

Or how about the following: rather than dropping bombs, these nations should get in a bus, drive over to the border of their enemy, ask permission to enter, be allowed to enter, and let's say they sit themselves down in a hospital. Then they would gather the people and say to them:

"Who among you will slash your wrists, because we are very angry! Not all of us here, but most of us are quite angry. Frankly, a few of us would rather be at home right now, but our bosses, who couldn't make it on this trip, have ordered us to come here to demand that you slash your wrists because our god is great, or else we will do it for you. Even though we are not 100% interested in slashing your wrists. A few of us would like to, however. About ten of us. Because we would like to get you back for that attack last week. No it doesn't matter who suffers for our retribution. So who will step forward? Show us your babies!"

Show us your boobies?

Ha-ha.

You say nothing about processing your own emotions.

My emotions were burned away long ago. Here is what I say. The violence stops with me.

Abdelaziz had stopped talking. Muhammad kept listening to the empty line. Then he listened to the dial tone. Then he listened to the empty line again. He imagined a hundred thousand arguments coming to him through the wire. He imagined the violence and the retribution. He imagined the endless cycle of the violence whirlpool. He imagined a whirlpool so wide that the foaming sides were taller than the walls of a city, with trucks, guns, and missiles thrown into the fray with entire hospitals, with women in birkhas, with women in g-strings, with tattooed muscle men raping and beating them, with tattooed muscle men raping and beating each other, eating chili cheese fries smothered in hummus and olives, drenched in crude oil, mixed with blood, getting shot for driving, getting shot minding their own business, getting shot for believing, for getting imprisoned, for getting caught forgetting where to be found in accordance with the law, with the Koran, with the Bible, with the Haftorah, for speaking the wrong language at the wrong time, in the wrong country. He imagined a giant spinning whirlpool with a tiny, pointed tip at the bottom that was so far down, so black, so empty, so void of any mass, of any reason, so void of any conviction, a dark and negative space so absorbing, so compelling that any mortal would be forced to dive toward it should one witness it, the eye of the storm, the crux of the void so negative, so hollow, that there would always be room for one more to fill it.

That was what Muhammad's conversation with Abdelaziz had left him with. He was convinced that under no circumstances, from now on, should he ever answer the telephone. He ripped the cord out of the wall decorated with flowery wallpaper. Then, he concentrated with all his might to erase the potentiality of another phone to reappear. He went through every permutation, should a telephone be delivered to his porch, or should one somehow assemble itself over the period of several days in his tool closet, or should the utensils in his kitchen drawer randomly amount to the equivalent of a telephone. He erased every possibility of manifesting a new telephone in his private sanctuary, even if by accident.

Muhammad's prison sentence lasted another full year, maybe more. He enjoyed his painful silence. Then he heard machine gun fire and grenades at the main gate, then outside his building, more down the hall, and then finally, the guns arrived at his cage.

When I Was Young

Steamships would clutter our front porch, up to the doorstep, washed to the house like so much driftwood. The captains, dizzy as fallen leaves, would yell up to me in my bedroom, asking for directions, my elbows draped over the windowsill horizon. Not all of them asked. Some found their own way. But the sea was far from where we lived.

Our porch collected the daggers of prostitutes, which had run off into the night, witless of their owners, scampering down the gutter, washing to our doorstep. Murder was a wildfire. The duels were performed with intimacy in sweaty alleys of stone pavers and wrought iron. Ladies or gentlemen, it did not matter. Their lives were expendable but never their honor. *Stilettos* and *facónes*. Scissors and comb points. The weapons fled when they could, out of disgust for their use. Blood lived in pools and never dried in some places.

The prostitutes kept company under a cone of oily street light, descending from a single lamp on the corner, quietly buzzing in the darkness, fixed to a leaning wooden pole, a pit stop at the edge of town. Ready for orgasm or death, any kind of titillation.

Every night, our streets rang with howling ghosts. Once, a

family had to leave their house because it had become so infested, they could no longer survive. It began with cups that wouldn't stay on the counter and cabinets spitting open. Then, it grew to flooding bathrooms, wardrobes hurled to the bed, window panes shattering, and then ceaseless sobbing in the walls. The activity did not subside once the family left. The obnoxious spirits stayed on and had their way with the place. They tore bricks from the fireplace, planks from the floor, boards from the ceiling, and hurled them across the house. People would collect and watch from the street. That's how impressive it was. The ghosts pumped energy into the lightbulbs intermittently, making the windows glow and the rooms swirl as debris flew, a cataclysm of breaking glass.

Magistrates and pilots and constables swam to our porch, floating down the street only to get caught in our hedges and roll up the walkway. So much fallout, so many stories. No discussions, only shouts of statistics and systems for a society that was controlled by people and not words; by words alone, and not the people. The people versus the bombs. With policy. Without policy. With an iron fist. With a leather glove. With an open hand. With the children dead. With the children educated. Hospitals for everyone. Hospitals for no one. Hospitals for some people. Cities in the sky with the walls up. Cities on the Earth with the walls down.

The flotsam was endless. Anything came to our front yard. My brain was a life raft. I barely clung to the side of an abysmal pool. For stability, I knit the hides of panthers together with jackals to make fiercer monsters; lean, black, silent killers with long fangs and eyeballs that glowed red in the dark, deep in the rosebush jungle vines.

Nana, our neighbor across the street, would occasionally and maybe accidentally, leave her dog poop in a paper bag on our porch. It arrived as anything else did in those days, as did Lala her dog. She came scampering to the porch, tongue out, wanting to be pet, kicking past the eyeballs and knives and steamships innocently enough, for she had no idea where her poop might have ended up, or what kind of a place it was, or how they got there.

Nana's laugh sounded much like her dog's bark, and her dog barked often, and Nana loved to laugh. Sometimes, Nana would see something funny on television and start laughing, which would make Lala a bit nervous, so she would bark and bark, and when she barked, she would often make backward sneezes. She couldn't help it. Nana explained this to me one morning on the sidewalk. She told me it was the cutest thing. Nana thought her dog's sneezing was the funniest sound ever.

So if Nana should start laughing for any reason, and cause Lala to bark, with Lala's strains of barking and backward sneezing bringing on uncontrollable peals of laughter from Nana, who would snort to catch her breath, it would in turn alarm the poor dog. They would go on like that, hour after hour, until Nana was sore, and there was a commercial on, and Lala would curl up on her pillow to sleep it off. And Nana would leave the couch to change her underwear.

I caught sight of her once, on her way over, with a paper bag in her hand. I went downstairs to tell dad. "Pop, Nana's on her way with more poop!"

"No she's not." He didn't even raise his head. He was sitting at the dining table in the late afternoon on a Saturday. He was peering deep into the wooden surface of the table, through his glasses. They were thick and thumb-smudged, with gold rims. "C'mere boy. You've got a booger."

"That's just my nose."

"No it's not. C'mere and let me have a look at that."

"But Nana!"

"Never mind her." He took me by the back of the head and pushed his finger into my nostril. I could feel the ridges of his skin.

Dad's finger smelled like garlic and soil. "I don't get it. What are you doing up in that room of yours, boy?" I didn't answer. He wasn't really asking.

MISSIVES

MLLE R. R. MAY BE AWARE
OF COMMUNICATIONS

Dear Mr. Leggett,

Before I begin, I must notify you that Mademoiselle in question will occasionally peruse any envelope at the mail table, as she has permitted herself to use my office key at her leisure. She therefore has every opportunity to monitor our communications.

Have we anything to hide? I suppose not.

That being said, life in the trenches is absorbing to the worst degree. The daily crossfire, a normal occurrence, takes on my utmost and yet most unnecessary considerations. It especially hurts when such interferences do not actually deserve my attention. I am forced to undertake my routines under the smoke-enriched sun as a disheveled monster. Aghast, agog, groping for normalcy, as if it ever existed.

I mean to say that an episode may take place, and even after the company has dealt with it, such an unending spell of self-reflection is cast upon the incident, that even the tiniest crackling of rifle fire wakes me up at night with a chest full of beating heart and the sweats.

To one degree, it is well within my nature. I accept that such considerations can be of genetic or chemical origin. To a second degree, I observe that these reactions manifest in phasic episodes, each one building, then gathering, then the total becoming vitally consuming, and without warning, it all ebbs into background noise. War, on a quotidian basis, is an invisible wave of sheer torment. To a third degree, and perhaps the more interesting, is that there may be a cosmic rationale. You see, on waking at odd hours of the morning, I have perceived the lights of other foxholes illumined—indicating they too may have had adequate cause to wrest themselves from the bedcovers and seek solace on the cool kitchen floor.

I awoke and stumbled out of bed just as they had, although I was not disturbed by any sound from neighboring apartments. I can not help but believe that they were stricken by a similar invisible stress—which brings me to the question—does insomnia travel in clouds over us, lumbering like a cosmic slug, from block to block, quietly sucking up Morpheus' sand?

Despite the aforementioned ideas, I find the whole thing derogating and unnecessary. I conceive of the plans lost and the brigades unplanned or unassembled due to my continual confusion over simple daily situations or personal affronts. I fear my service could be shortened because of it. Were it not that I feel I have more to share with the world than it will currently allow!

A tour of these foxholes would reveal to you: soldiers tripping over their reflection in mud puddles, soldiers barking blindly into the air, ululating names of their dead trench mates. Then there is the one who wanders in a circle with a stack of rifles over his shoulder. He is sadly hilarious in his routines, but aren't we all. One is only as mad as his concept of madness will allow.

But the War is endless, Mr. Leggett. My better soldiers shoot at the chin of daylight. Their bullets catch fire in the blaze of the sun. May each bullet be blessed on its way to whomsoever may stop its path, be they God, enemy, or patriot.

My sharpshooters fire into the belly of the dark. Their bullets strike targets cold and sharp like icicles. They drag stars down from the sky and shape it into massive concentric cones, drilling it into the torso of individuals lucky enough to be nullified at the mercy of my delivering soldiers.

And the shapes made by stars, ripped from the night sky as our bullets pass through it, form the letter *V* over and over for *Victory*, at whose breast every last one of us would love to suckle. Or they are *Z*s for *Zarathustra* who promised us diminishment in life and a brutal ungodly end in the afterlife. Lastly they become *W*s for *why?* As in *why for* or *why come* or *why stop*?

My people and my equipment continually disappoint me. And so does my *self*. And the tears will not spill, yet I call to them silently as I prostrate myself to the exquisite power every evening before I make my next miserable attempt at *sleep*.

So I propose finally, that if God is smiling, is this base existence all there was ever meant to be? Is it all just *this*?

Or, if God is *intending* to smile, then where can we, as reasonable men and women, auspiciously place ourselves, and which are the acts that we are to perform to best *entice* him to smile upon us?

I don't give two shakes of a little lamb's tail who reads this letter any more. Perhaps it will be the shameless and nosy Mademoiselle. If she finds intrigue on my bureau, she is obviously too boring to expose an international secret. Should she share this letter, may its squalid lines offer the readers some modicum of protection against the continuum of silence and torrential delirium.

I await your answer along with the supplies I have ordered. It remains unseasonably chilly here at the front.

Best Regards,

Group Captain Y

THE LAMB'S BLOOD

August 4, 1975

Dear Nephew,

The blood of the lamb we slew on the day of your birth flowed profusely. It was a deeper red than usual and poured from our courtyard to bless the neighboring houses. Then it blanketed the tiny streets of our city ankle deep in thick purple mud, stopping traffic and soaking pedestrians.

The blood moved in floes. It heaped itself in corners and mounded against buildings in drifts and congealed there. It buried front doorsteps, rising to the flower boxes. It was decided that the houses with blood up to the windows belonged to the luckier families.

Over the following days, the blood was carefully scooped away and saved. They said it brought *baraka*, good fortune. It was shaped and fired into the hand of Fatima for protection and bowls for ablutions. They made cups and plates out of it, but soon there were warnings not to use them. People were going crazy with delight from exposure to the ceramics, a sort of drug-induced euphoria.

It was said that the clay belonged to the devilish djinn of the dirt and had not been officially requisitioned by the townspeople who were thereby subject to any kind of attack when in proximity of their ceramics. After all, blood is half earth and half ocean, so the permissions can be unclear. The djinn are known to wait for a person to use an earthen path, for instance, crossing the courtyard on the way to the bathroom at night, when they slip under the skin of the human and claw them to death from the inside out. The djinn can also kill slowly, by putting a disease into the flesh so limbs fall off, one by one, year after year.

Other victims are stricken in their sleep. They are found in the morning, having strangled their lovers and themselves. To prevent this kind of disaster, people broke their plates and buried them. But some people chose to hide them. They saved a few pieces each. They were beautiful. The ceramics were famous for their peculiar dark purple hue, and perfectly smooth, for the clay had no grains. It was as pure a material as any fine glass or china. For the safety of the ceramics and the families, they were nervously tucked into crawlspaces under the houses, but above the ground, to remain out of reach of the dirt djinn.

Then we heard rumors of secret late night parties. Couples and groups would lay with one another in candlelight and serve milk and *sellu* on the plates and spoon it into one another's mouth. The gatherings would grow close and swelter, as if they had been smoking kif. The lights would grow dim on their own. And the pillows and the sheepskins laid over the carpets on the floor would warm and soften. And the incense would burn and bring the walls in closer, just as the air would hang thick under the released excitement. Skin of male and female became revealed and may have also touched. Then drums and singing and dancing would ensue, accompanied by laughter and caresses within the blinding air, caused by a smoldering less from the candles and more from the dancing bodies in the depth of night.

Yet, the purple stain on those plates and cups will always be ignored. Families hand them down as heirlooms, or they manage to escape of their own volition, tempting the taker, snatched by thieves, or the wretched djinn of the dirt. The results of that clay used to be in the newspaper regularly, and we still hear about it today. Unfortunate newlyweds, who do not know the origins of, or why to never use these dark and exquisite ceramics, are left victim to the blood that flowed in your honor. Your blood. The happiness of this city is forever marred by the black magic of your blood.

August 8, 1975

But my father, your grandfather, pulled a talisman from the belly of the lamb—a solid piece of wound-up grass, formed like a man, with arms and legs and a head. It was deemed good. A good time to be born. A good time to celebrate. The winter of your birth was dry, but rains soon fell in the mountains and fattened our rivers. We hung the meat high, testicles out, to be admired and to drain completely.

Mother says there were such mounds of couscous that it burst from the pots it was cooked in. But I don't remember. We filmed this day. Someone filmed it. I don't know who had the camera. Maybe you did. The newborn. You were so far away and we heard of your birth almost by accident.

You were born, they cleaned you up and brought you home, then months later, probably as an afterthought, your father quietly called my father. So we celebrated. We ate our fresh-brined olives and bread, and the couscous, and we slaughtered a lamb for you. Same as they would for any of us. Same as they did for me twenty months before. But no one filmed it.

I want you to know that I hate you. I hate you as if you were my twin, even though we are more than a year apart. I hate you! You are like a brother, but I am your uncle. You are my nemesis. I am you the way you *ought to be*. I know how to do things right, so much better than you. I will keep the tradition properly.

I saw you in that film! I swear I saw your shadow swimming there, the American bastard, lolling in the currents of blood as it touched our neighbors' doorsteps! That fresh wry look of the little baby spirit they were all so proud of—*welcome to us, welcome to the world!* was the song we sang for you. But I saw that smirk you carried. I smelled it too, oh it smelled like a rotting skunk, rising within the fumes of the roasted lamb, when it was served after prayer, and before dancing. My brothers offered me chunks of the beast, but it was rotten with your smirk—that same smirk you showed up in thirty years later, and for the first time!

The responsibility of taking care of your father fell to me, since you wouldn't come. In his final years, he gave up hope in retrieving you. The far flung seed from the increasingly inconceivable horizon. I called once he died. No one else would have told you. I spoke. You tried to. There was nothing to say. For us, for him, his death was a relief. He'd been sick for fifteen years. I'll show you where he is buried, should you return.

You haven't seen the film. You may never see it. You tell us you will, but we think you do not plan on coming back.

Personally, I don't care if I never hear from you again, but please write to your family at least once in a while.

Sincerely,

Your Uncle

Living In Fog

Diary of The Last Days of Forrest Pike Brougham III, Deckhand;
H.M.S. Gouliot.

December 17, 1826

Living in fog is more difficult than it would seem. Our course was laid before we began. The crew has been asking questions, but our Captain remains confident. It is neither dark nor light here, with little differentiation between sea and sky. Confusion offers itself to us at every angle, to anyone who might be swept up by it. The Captain keeps the ship's nose pointed at the compass and we manage to drift at a leisurely pace. We are reassured that his crowded charts hold us fast in their matrix.

But this fog is beleaguering. To see it, one would think any direction the same as the last. I could be here or on shore, at my mother's or my sister's. At night, the ship is festooned with lanterns. They billow out gold in ten-foot globes. One might think us a parade ship, but we keep them lit to avoid collision.

December 18

There's adequate wind to take us further, but home could be eons away. Looking to sea, I imagine it is sky. Above is below, but not perfectly so. The water's dumb mockery of the sky is amusing. It wishes to be still, but blisters and horns erupt nonetheless. The water emotes and cavorts uncontrollably—St. Vitus' dance.

You, Water, are the darker brother to Sky; more braggart, freighted with worry, prone to violence. Air, too, is unwieldy, but never Sky. Sky is ever the calm observer, the elder brother.

December 19

We raced through the hams and the sheep we brought with us. We ate the last of our turkeys days ago, and now, Johannes' monkey is looking tasty. Some are mentioning the meat on the back of its thighs. Late in the evening, I eat from a bowl of rotted beans that I've saved. It sickens me to ingest, but I'm sated for hours. I leave the others to their stale old rum. But I'm killing that monkey tomorrow if I get the chance.

Sky, divorced of its wretched brother, Wind, is a peaceful mate. We convene regularly, as I plod through my chores under its velvet canopy. The fog hasn't left us for thirty days, and land could be just off the bow. They'd never let us know how twisted we are. We must keep trusting the Captain's reckoning. The world looks the same—whether you're standing on your head or drowning in the ocean—after a month or so, of drifting in the fog.

Christabel, O Christabel!

Why won't the words come?

> *Your hand locked in mine*
> *you and I walking forever*
> *on plains so verdant!*
> *The country receives us!*
> *O Christabel!*

The King has ordered artesian waters from those muddy primitives of the Americas. Our frigate is encumbered with a load in its hold of no less than fifty barrels of the infernal stuff.

> *Christabel, O Christabel!*

I wonder if I will ever get this poem written—

> *My blood is a tiny sea*
> *modeled in red!*
> *It pulses and slams*
> *the shores of my skin*
> *in your honor!*

> *The waves swell and heave*
> *in concert to the muse*
> *of your name—*

A hundred times have I put pen to paper to rattle this ode, decrying my hapless passion for your soul! But I'll write it eventually. I swear on my grave that at least I'll scratch out the rhythm of this marvelous treatise I have so longed to finish!

December 22

O Christabel, the days here are waterlogged from dawn to dusk. I've kept a bowl of beans served up three weeks ago, now gone bad. Something in their process of desiccation has been hampered by our moist environment. Small growths of blue fur have sprouted within. All I need do is ingest the tiniest fraction and volumes of information are revealed to me.

Here! I take it thus, a thumb- and forefinger-full, I say, it is getting powerfully heady. I vomit into the sea from my porthole, emptying my innards into the very chasm that has swallowed everything I ever loved or strived for. No! The sea does not care. It absorbs the great or small. I watch it go as we progress. My vomit pools in pitiful foaming spots. I watch them dip and twist like doilies on the glassy surface below. The ocean is fat and grey, old and not wise, fair Christabel.

Ah! My mind opens. As if the top of my head has been lifted. Now I understand everything. I might be the only one, but I think I can see the solemn faces of those three bastard brothers: Sea, Sky, and Air. Yes. Today they are triplets. Identical in shape, age and form. Sky is the calm one, not freighted with worry or chatter like his heavier brother, Sea. Air, or Wind, as he is known, is the traitor. Prone to violent outbursts, he's a friend one minute and the next he's got you tight by the throat.

Sea just doesn't care. He'll join in any time he likes. But, it's all he can do, Sky, to sit and watch. For that, they are bastards, each of them, either cooperating to pummel us or, as now, acting the one as absent as the other. The best we can do is sit here and ride our feeble speck of bark in the half-light.

Christabel, I've been trying for days to finish your poem. It must be complete before we make landfall. "O, Christabel!" I'll proclaim, and this name will be the toast of the town! Our nation will rise in unison to chant my verses! Damn it if I don't need another chew of the blue bean mixture! The entire universe opened up to me the first time I ate it.

And we, we have eaten nearly everything on the ship. We started out with a dozen turkeys. We boiled them, ate them, returned our scraps to the pot and boiled them up again, spiced with dry turnip greens from the cook's garbage. We made twenty soups out of the cook's garbage. No one is allowed to throw anything overboard, lest we're able to make a soup out of it. We're using the King's precious water and now we've boiled our every last bit of trash to survive. Yes, Johannes' stupid monkey is looking quite nice by now. Fat little thighs on that thing, indeed!

> *O Christabel!*
> *My blood*
> *is a sea that thrashes endlessly*
> *against the shores of my flesh for you!*
>
> *My heart*
> *slams against the hull of my chest*
> *in your name!*
>
> *My ribs*
> *are but prison bars*
> *if I can't have you!*

My heart
is but chained by my arteries
if I can't have you!

My heart
begs to fly free to your side!
But Hell!

I'll never get your poem written. Christabel, the name of my niece's fawn. Yes—a deer. An animal. It was her pet, back in Cordova. Who would know or care anyway? Once they hear my magical script, invoking the name of a wretched deer my niece saved from starvation. My brother and his cohorts scooped it up whilst gorging themselves on the ecstatic spoils of the hunt—the hanging, the bleeding, the skinning, the chopping of the mother, the parting-out of the mother. And how they feasted on her! How they ate her in forty ways as my niece nursed her fawn! "We'll fatten it up and set it loose on the property," said my brother. The fool! Lying to his child—"Have some more beef roast, sweetheart!" Sweet-HART, rather!

O Christabel,
my eyes are useless
without you to fill them.

And useless indeed, as Sky here blends right into Water. Air too, is constant. We move, aye, but Lord knows where the current leads.

December 24, Christmas Eve

Oh, Christabel. If you only knew where your mother was. Hark! Someone is coming! I stumble through my chores every day like an automaton, but today I have been hiding in my bunk. Shhht! They pass. I'll go out. But I will return my sweet! No mortal shall tear me away from you. None!

Here we are again my love, as we are meant to be, but in prayer. Tonight is the Silent Night.

December 25, Christmas Day

The bastard brothers enclose us still. Lanterns fixed to the bow, glowing ten feet in every direction. One would think us a wedding barque come evening, but hélas no gaiety blesses our ship. We've lit them at our Captain's behest to alert incomers to our presence. So we don't get smashed. But I'll be smashed any day of the week for you, fair Christabel!

> *Christabel, O Christabel!*
> *The frogs of shore sing your name!*
> *They chirp in such harmony!*
> *They float on night air, flying under the wind!*
> *I'll punish every criminal for bellowing out of turn!*
> *For they can never know the attitudes of love you are due my maiden!*
>
> *The trees, they whisper your legend among themselves.*
> *The rain, embarrassed by my clarity of vision for you,*
> *will bury itself in the soil, sneaking down to the lake*
> *where we float.*
>
> *Christabel, O Christabel!*
> *Lightning snags the air and explodes for want*
> *of the words I put down in your honor!*

Were I but a playing card, the nature of my royal station
would never comply to a worldly dynasty
so well placed as your own.
For your tiniest denomination trumps me.
It is thus, O Christabel!

There! Those lines are perhaps not too bad. The last stanza stretches it a bit, however.

December 28

Let it be known that the owner of the ship, the man who hired our Captain, had promised the King several barrels of Artesian water from those foul natives of New India. The claim was that it would revive his health and return his mental faculties. So today, we are effectively drowning in fog, lost in the water without a sky to direct us, and burdened no less, with a cargo of water.

Shore could be ten yards away and we'd never know. We're just as trapped as if there were no such thing as land. We've almost wiped out our stores of food, so we boil what we have, return the scraps to the pot and boil them ad-infinitum, dropping in novelties like boots and gloves and rope trimmings for fiber. We may never run out of water to pilfer. We may never run out of water to tread upon.

December 31, A Dream

Oh Christabel, our eyes are as full as our stomachs on nothing but grey soup. Hélas. I sleep:

—I can't tell. Has it stopped raining? I see the puddles trembling.

There's a hole in the clouds. Now a lower cloud, a massive one, has caught the moon's direct glare. It is suspended, silent, ambulant. This is an unfamiliar sky. It is brawny and scattered. The moon carves a path between several layers of cloud; each one bulky and muscular, and disorganized enough to let a few, straight, silver fingers touch the grass before me.

A cry pierces the low clouds passing. It is a yell, a yowl. Plaintive. The clouds unfold to reveal a perfectly minted moon. The red eye of Taurus stares down from a heaving black cave. The sound is not a rogue drunk or a couple's squabble. It is two cats. They bellow in the dark under the passing clouds, and as they attack, they tear one another to shreds. Memories of blood run through the streets. Somehow, I know this is heaven. I stare at the moon, expecting to be drawn up to it.

Where am I? What is this land? Yes, it is familiar. At once, I know. This is my fate. Somewhere within the grass, squirm the sand dunes and fog. Somewhere in the sky, vultures fly over the sea. Here lives a naked, craggy butte, kicking mist over its shoulder. It has a thirst for blood, for souls. It needs to kill or damage the humans that clamber upon it—

I awake to the sensation that my pillow is full of beetles. Lifting my head, I realize my pillow is tightly wrapped around my face.

January 7, 1827

About today? What can I say about today. The weather is the same. We cruise gently across a hazy mirror. But the Captain's floor, above my cabin, betrays a canopy of chattering clocks, punctuated with the wheeze and creak of our flexing ship. The ocean cradles the hull about me. It wraps and oozes, now squeezing, now pulling our frame in the vertical, now horizontal. The limits of my skull ride the measures of the clocks' continual song of no melody, no refrain, only a brace of unsynchronized calibrations. It is a rain, rather, of machinery and ticking. Confusion voiced and boundlessly random.

January 10

At evening, when the day's shifts have settled and all have retired, each rolling in his bunk, the clocks play a ticking song that permeates the root of my quarters. I understand it now as my dirge.

The ship's hull provides a sawing counter bass. The slippery tides form a chorus, and the numerous clocks in the Captain's room, above, provide a poignant section of staccato flutes. These flutes are tumultuous; like confused animals. Hiding, conniving, judging, they belie any hint of rhythm, discordant as a group of human heartbeats. The only pattern binding them is that they worry for safety together.

This is the music I sleep to. Certain nights I'm forced to stop my ears with wads of cloth. But the arcing counter bass rides me to the bone! I am forced to bear witness to the extent of their symphony.

It is a music that never ends, only rambles the night through. Soon enough, I am rousted back to my duties. The spinning of days is the only regular drumbeat to guide me, every night dipping back into cacophony. "That SOUND!" I cry, muffled in my bedsheets. Chewing at the blankets, I thank the bloody spray of stars above, all be they hidden from me for an eon, that at least I am dry.

January 24

Johannes' stupid monkey slid off his shoulder and straight into the water today. Probably fainted from starvation. Never mind; we'll not hesitate to throw Johannes into the soup once he dies of grief for the thing. The sorry bastard. I am so hungry for solid food, I would eat the callouses off my heels if they were only dressed in brown gravy with a side of roasted beets.

My bowl is not missed by the cook. No one cares about a missing dish. Curious though, the beans have shifted in it. I do believe a colony of beetles has grown upon them. Well, they don't eat it so fast. Maybe they've always been there. Perhaps their presence aids in the fermentation process. I need smaller amounts lately, as the strength seems to have increased. At once I must set myself to work—

> *Christabel, O Christabel!*
> *Your perfumed curls, your willowy limbs*
> *dance in my mind like faeries of the forest!*

> *Artemis and Diana*
> *heroines both, but nothing like you are my grace!*
> *They bow in your honor, they hand over ribbons*
> *and dress you in their garlands.*

> *Christabel, O Christabel!*
> *We belong together under the smiling eyes*
> *of God! Oh how we'll dance on our wedding day!*

> *Our love is boundless my dear, our whisperings of truth*
> *will knit the canopy of God's heaven*
> *with the purest ebullience!*

> *Call to me in the open daylight!*
> *Let the silvery mists of love twirl about us as we dance*
> *down the river valley from the wedding chapel!*

> *We'll make our way to a snug cabin*
> *with a roaring fire and lace curtains about the windows!*

From there, we'll usher three children into the world
and I will ensure we have meals on the table
by selling wood crafts to the town
from a little shop on the corner!

Meat pies for the young ones!
Now is time for schoolbooks and such!
We are swimming in joy
and the tides of our love grow
with each passing year.

Christabel, O Christabel!
I am only ever yours
on Earth as it is in Heaven.

There! Christabel! Is this your poem? Have I done it? Let me see. I'll read it back from the start. Is it moving enough? That's the real question. Away to sleep for now. How silly of me. I must have eaten a beetle instead of the beans. The effect is more powerful. Did I eat a beetle? All the same. By now the mixture is probably equal parts. No wonder I'm dreaming of beetles!

January 27

My dreams were more intense this night. I was cutting clouds with a knife. I was alone in a grand house, waiting for a clockwork chimney to strike the hour. I couldn't count the chimes. They were puffs of smoke. My work is affected. A ray of sunlight poured through the fog and almost burned me alive for an instant. I mentioned it to no one. Here I must admit; every day I am feeling more comfortable in the fog. Should it clear I'll probably swaddle my head with a sheet. I can do my tasks with my eyes closed anyway.

February 10

I haven't written in two weeks. Now I believe the Captain is my father. He has no clocks. Why did I want him to have clocks? So much ringing and ticking. The clocks! It must be the shadow of authority, filtering down through the cracks of the floorboards! The mechanical fist of dominance! The unfaltering and rigorous ticking of time! Christabel, Oh Christabel! I whimper your name, and I feel you're waiting for me to finish you, but we both know it can never be!

This man, the Captain, is my father! He brought me here. He must have! He brought me up a soldier then a sailor! —But why? Why am I so poor about decks? Why else would I hate it so very much? Christabel, you know me better. My niece might have named you, but it was I who plucked you from Coleridge! I mutated and evolved you into a greater goddess than his frustrated mind could ever invent! His words were callous! Un-heartfelt! Confined! Mine are free! I am free and am liberated! Here! Thus! It is clearly a family of beetles now living on the remains of my bean curd.

A snaggle of blind, wretched, writhing little apostrophes, stealing my liberating invention, my tool of creativity! I'll just take another one of your children now and, thank you! I am free again! No blankets of time holding me back from launching myself to heaven if I so desire! They get me dizzier and more airborne each one that I chew! I'm sure I could float away home if I tried! By God, their bodies have distilled the mixture by power of digestion! They are tiny wandering stomachs! Fleshy wine casks! They will be my salvation! Christabel! Oh! Christabel! The three bastard brothers are stacked, one upon the other, in three unbroken lines! The very symbol of solid stillness! My heavens, they beckon! More children! I – must – F L Y !

~ ~ ~*~ ~ ~

Chantey:
   Young Sailor Brougham
   Far away from home
   Took 'is life alone
   when 'e jumped into the foam.

Chorus:
   Oh, Young Sailor Brougham
   Jumped into the foam
   Ali' alive-O
   An' ne'er made it home!

   Young Sailor Brougham
   Seven Seas did 'e roam
   ate the blue bean bowl
   An' 'e ne'er finished 'is poem!

Chorus Repeat:
   Oh, Young Sailor Brougham
   Jumped into the foam
   Ali' alive-O
   An' ne'er made it home!

IDI AMIN KNEELS

Idi Amin kneels to pray at the tomb of Nusrat Fateh Ali Khan and,
moved to tears, utters an impromptu song of cosmic love. It is the
colossal meeting between two leaders, two larger-than-life forces of
humanity and inhumanity. Amin takes special care to call out each
syllable of the phrase *Allah—Akhbar!* Clutching at the grass below
him, he presses his forehead against the foot of the cool white steps.
He rises occasionally with his eyes closed:

"My lover's shawl flies upon the wind!

It was left haphazard by the shore on our lakeside walk.

It flutters like a bird and soars at times like an eagle.

It infuses cities, mountains, fields and gardens

With fertile perfumes of honey, lilac, milk, and musk.

A concoction of our devotion and loving caresses

Inspired only by your Immortal Song!

The perfume spreads bliss and peace and respect for Allah

Through the currents of air which envelop the fair landscape.

May the floral winds of love twirl about us now, sweet Fateh.

Teach me your magic! I know only the results of your spells and feel
like a hapless pawn

Trapped within greatness, forbidden from something greater.

Blow your ghost into my chest!

Share the wealth and the drive of your holy and profound career.

You made so many people so very happy.

That I might know love and power is undeniable

But I believe yours to be a love and a power

Wrapped more closely in the protective embrace of Allah.

Whisper to me now and guide me to the paths

Leading to God's sheltered gardens

Where fountains pour rosewater and grapes hang fat and warm and
so low

They climb by themselves into the mouths of lovers, as they roll past
in ecstatic union.

Where women lounge unveiled amongst cavalcades of brightly
colored flowers

Spanning two palms' width each, yawning bold stripes of all hues.

Stamens like tongues, standing unfurled and unashamed.

Where men are free to lose themselves in divine contemplation

Awash in roaring waves of abandonment

Granted by the simultaneous recitation

Of all verses of the Koran, which form a harmonious galactic tapestry

As broad and as colored as the flowers of the garden, as simple and as
complex as the many shawls

Dropped by the maidens therein, which form a cosmos as contoured
as the bodies they hid.

A simultaneous recitation revealing the holy scriptures as evoked by
a chorus of millions

Yet condensed as one prismatic multidimensional Truth held in
diamond

Pronouncing the singular resonant voice of Allah, al-hamdoulaylah."

Idi Amin wipes his head. It is aglaze with tears and sweat. The wind
clips the tail of his white robes. The grass has two divots where his
knees have pressed. He kneels again before turning away.

"Hear me now and educate me with the aid of Muhammad the
Prophet!

May my life end as fruitful as thine. Insha'allah.

God took you too soon from us the living. The ugly. The struggling.

Show me the way."

PROPHECIES

The Talking Sticks
and the Archaeologists—
A Tale of Random Values

It had recently been retrieved, from a cave beneath the black fountains of Nuyt, in the northern plains of Afghanistan: an assemblage of sticks with curious markings at each end. The sticks were found in a stone jar that had been placed within the chest of an ox and thus, mummified. It was thought, by the archaeologists who found them, that the sticks had been left in the the ox as part of a rite to commemorate a holy gambling game known to be played among an exclusive sect of elders in the prehistoric community.

The people of this culture were impressive architects and agrarians. They fed their steer a diet of flowers and grasses that varied according to changes in weather patterns. This diet produced a fine quality of meat that nourished everyone, but the heart was reserved to bolster the strength of their warriors.

The warriors, whose broad chests bore thick tattoos of totem animals, were somehow controlled in battle by the elders like stringless puppets. Among the few rock paintings that have been found are scenes that indicate either the ferocity or immortality of the warriors, perhaps both. Their uncanny connection to the elders is depicted by showing them engaged in acts of war, held by giant thin hands connected to unnaturally long arms. The arms lead back to the elders hidden in a bank of trees, seething with fog.

These people revered gambling. They had brought the game to new spiritual heights and tragically, to a level where it may have even affected their destiny. Scrolls found tucked into the cave walls recount a period of time when their obsession with games of chance caused them to forecast the future again and again. Each time resulted in a different outcome.

Confusion over the foretelling process or misinterpretations of their destiny ensured their demise by causing arguments, in-fighting, and finally, frantic spates of murder, as the opposing camps grew from two, to four, and splintered off again to sixteen, sixty-four, and so on.

⁓

The archaeological team had come to the conclusion at the initial discovery, that the sticks were peculiar samples because they were outfitted with inscriptions found nowhere else at the dig and as far as they knew, nowhere else in time.

The archaeologists succeeded in publishing their findings in a popular scientific journal. Never could they have fathomed that their prehistoric objects would resemble a contemporary system. It was only by chance that a genetics technician happened to read their article, which reported the team's conclusions, accompanied by a few sketches and photographs.

Overwhelmed with excitement, the genetics technician wrote to the authors, explaining that the patterns on the sticks resembled a system his colleagues had devised to differentiate moss genotypes.

They had been comparing mutation frequencies in a particular species and found it necessary to improvise a shorthand, based on chunks of DNA, charted according to their position and composition on the protein chain. Instead of listing each amino acid individually, specific regions of DNA were identified and assigned a symbol.

⌒

This news helped the archaeologists immensely. They received the list of symbols via email within two hours. Using substitutions for confusing or eroded markings on the sticks, they improved the labels, but something was wrong. The archaeologists arranged the sticks in order of size and could not make sense of the markings. Then they arranged them according to the markings but failed, because the two sides wouldn't match up. Did they need to match up? No one knew. They were adrift in possibility and potential, facing the most dramatic archaeological discovery in centuries, from an amazing site that produced new enigmas at every turn, with a pile of schematics and artifacts that led only to more questions.

In frustration, someone threw the sticks on a table. Playfully, and familiar with pre-literate games of chance, someone else wrote the value of that first throw. An impromptu game erupted, and the scientists discovered that random values were the missing ingredient to understanding the symbols. This was their eureka moment.

Looking back at the original email, they re-labelled the sticks to more closely represent the symbols used by the other lab. The system also had an alphabetic equivalent. They soon found that by tracking the results of several throws, and writing down the letters, words came out. From these words, a voice emerged. They called that voice The Oracle. It seemed to be a dark spirit. Part of what that voice spoke is transcribed here:

Breaking clouds suffer whiteout sky tornado

Do not fear me for the terms of my love
are only sharply.
Yet take no heed of the hundred thousand thousand
twirling knives of my arms for they adore you.
And leave they only slim bruises
of knowledge.

Hide thee plainly in sight as we smite thee.
Take the wrath of my penance on thy legless torso.
Wander directly from the engagement.
Engagement in my fog-like vision.

Cast we now blood up to her arms.
Join us separately and we engage thee.
Take us individually into thy mouth and speak us.
Take us apart and split us knowingly.

Knowing lovingly bind us all the few leavings
the wanderers.
Do not forget that what I say
is already of you.
For I only reiterate you.
And I am you. In that I was you.

ALCHEMY OF VOWELS

We dream of traveling the universe—but is not
the universe within ourselves? At present this realm
seems so dark, so lonely, so shapeless.
—JoHannus "Tree" Gerthy, Billy Master, 1975

The following is an Alchemy of Vowels as seen by the Divinator
Clemcroft "Novalis of the Hills" Hardenberg, *Miskallaneous*
Observayshuns, 1998:

A is for the apple jack li'l Susie's been chuggin' and how it sends her to
the windy cliffs yellin' at the top of her lungs. "A" is for the moment
when her toe is outstretched, pointed at the middle of nuthin'. Darin'
us she'll jump.

E is the ball of yarn Gramma uses to knit our hats every winter. "E" is
the fact that the hats never change and always tend to unravel when
we need 'em. "E" is also the reality of her threat that she'll stuff one
down yer throat for cursin'.

I is for the darkness of the land after sunset. "I" is for the feeble lights of the houses gleamin' in the dark and a fear of the creatures that could attack you when you sleep. I dub "I" for the certainty that they will.

O is the tallest tree you can imagine. There's a dead pig strung up the side of it. It looks like an ordinary hunt as you approach, but the pack of critters lappin' up blood at the base of the tree is unlike any you ever laid eyes on. And your neighbors are in with 'em. That is the nature of "O."

U is the final and the darkest one of them all. "U" is a howl in the caverns of yer core. "U" is exactly why we make moonshine and why we call it that. "U" brings us back to "A". Hell, "U" is why we drink so much and shoot aerosol cans. "U" is why we love to watch fires burn and slow down for highway accidents.

ARISE AND CLIMB ALL LIVING FIVERS
In Fear of War, Prague, 1631

I. INTRODUCTION—*A plea for guidance in dire times*

This brings these lovers this brings these doubters.
For this is to the calling millions
The millions wretched the millions asking
Our hearts are breaking for written vespers.
And this tale will shake the stubborn breakers
Pine we now requesting guidance
Take us now we search we hunger
Now bring us vision. We lost the treadle.

II. THE FALSE PROPHET—*The town is courted by a man who offers only false hope. It ends in despair.*

Graven on the illuminated page
When did we once pursue a mage
And we admired his terrible age

Such fools as us loved a so-called sage.
He gave us warmth and we ran to greet him
He told of miracles that we'd complete him
He gave us knowledge and we'd entreat him
We took his blessing and dared not question.
"Let us all soar for the sky is a dream!
Let us call to God for he waits in the wings!
We will all be rich! The time is coming!
Your dues have been paid! Now start the drumming!"
His eyes flared wildly as he granted our wishes
And we rejoiced full fare in what he gave us
In rainbows and pastels it was all sugar sweetened
He cancelled our pains. He strengthened the weakened.
But it was always just our mind uneasy
And our prophet was an impostor
A feeble liar who led us nowhere.
Our town grew cold with all hope freezing.
Within the cold an ignorance grew
Like flaming metal overspilled in madness.
Oh down ye go unwinding spiral flicker
Freezing flames doused our hopeful trickle.

III. THE DEVICE—*In desperation, the Elders kidnap and drug a child, to create an Oracle.*

Yet hope we had searched was inside of us
Possibility all hung astride of us
Someone recalled the forbidden recipe
And now we set to make us a savior—
Choose us one from among the children
Break his or her ties with the village fellows

Wrap the subject in blankets and linens
And bring it to us in the dead of night.
Its power is past the umbilical
Beneath the blind of the physical
Exploring we thus the spiritual
Syphon we will the essential.
Roll it back on the bed we seeded the pillow
Dampen the noises 'til the outside is hollow
Vagaries weaken the senses and trust
Bring this youth to the dark and let us follow.
Drug the draught now and give it slow
We'll wait out the bells of the church tower
In quiet and calm let dialog narrow
As soon as we have it we'll witness the marrow.
And subtly comes the exquisite message
In ringing tones its contents emerges
Awaiting in silence we document all.
Cataleptic murmurs will give us the answers.

IV. THE ORACLE—*The unconscious child channels
the voice of a spirit.*

And not from the tongue or lips ungirded
Do the prophecies tumble in rhythmical riddles
And not from the throat for it gives only prattle
But we give ear to the sternum bringer of Truth.
And the chest of the youth goes on to say
Everything we could have dreamed of
And the colors are wide and various
The place ebbs and flows in front of us.
"Now give me your ears for I speak it thus

And do not test me for my temperament.
What I offer you is only words— not things.
Your fortune is up to yourselves you'll see."
Then the young form does some shaking
Until the bed and the floors are disturbed
And the entire apartments unraveled
With a vibrant and deafening hum.
"Taking the trouble to tie up your speaker
Will not but break you so much further
In witchcraft and occult you relinquish your magic.
Devices and methods distract you from truth.
You seek comfort but make complexity.
A colorful blanket is none the warmer.
In patterns and matrices you lose sight of your goal.
"But we have been so careful," someone mutters.
"All was done to the best capacity . . ."
"We meant no harm," was all one can remark.
Yet another dares to say:
"If all indeed, is up to question,
Then who are you; and say you what, from where,
To us, and for that much anyway . . .
Who are we?" The child grows pale
And shivers deeply within the wrappings.

v. THE VOICE—*The spirit describes itself. It was a leader long ago.*

"I am what was a voice of sincerity
From the ages when our people resembled
More the creatures of nature than humans.
I was a being of credence; a healer.
We dwelt in valleys buried our dead high

In the mountains deep at the end
Of caverns consecrated by forebears.
There in the black of the tunnels do I rest.
I am on a platform above the cave floor.
I am as is this child wrapped tightly
In linens and decorated with jewels
And I was as this child is used as a Device.
My eyes now removed have been replaced with
Wildflowers. My ears and mouth are stuffed
With saffron cinnamon and cardamom.
And thus I melt into the ether.
I listen to the wavering cosmos
It lifts and dances joining my body
And too much of it is revealed to me.
I stare through my eyeless skull— perceiving."

VI. THE ORACLE'S MORALITY TALE—*The Text, a fable*

"Before the final stroke of my heart
I heard a baby's cry— it was a male.
He was soft and his breath sweet and new.
He was a babe and not for he was a Text.
I see him through the eyes of his mother.
The Text is flexible interpretable.
He needs love caresses and bid for his will.
His shouts are glorious we marvel in pride.
And the Mother we are caring loving.
And the baby demanding fulfilling.
And we love it too much we wait for dying.
And dying for this love must be truly great.
And so the Text matures into Process.

And the Process begins its testing.
He's attempting situations different.
He's testing the strength of his upbringing.
And the baby comes home much older.
Ready for the loving he remembers.
He finds that everything is growing.
He calls for his mother and she's still there.
They speak of his youth and potential.
They speak of the babies the patterns born.
Growing every minute yet loved as if
The only one. Finding this truth they cry.
Crying they embrace and finding comfort
They see fit to climb upon one another.
They extract joys and feelings unexpected.
And after the Mother must kill herself.
The Text now expulsed wanders for nothing.
In his travels he inscribes his woes
At the foot of castles and churches he sees.
He finds the mark of others there.
He trods open fields crisscrossed by cannons.
Each bullet wrapped in Text and most older
Than he. For this he cries and the flowers
In my eyes take root and grow beautiful.
Only the Youth is flexible and yet
As he ages he sees it as weakness.
Adaptability mistaken for flimsy.
So often Youth makes one feel powerless."

VII. THE ANSWER — *The township is bewildered. The answer is too simple: commonality and community.*

Note: Humans are represented by the numeral 5: two arms, two legs, and a head.

And the rooms cease their movement.
And the gatherers sobbing quietly.
Someone mops the brow of the child.
Another raises the curtains to daylight.
Stunned, we mutter and disassemble
Staggering back to the streets of our houses.
A few of us murmur a song we know
For soothing the spirit from thundering storms.
We come back to our bedrooms and lay there
Quietly asking God for assistance
To take in what we had actually done
And pondering the last thing told to us.
Before leaving, the voice had said loudest
in a fit of vapor and torrent:
"Oh, arise and climb all living Fivers!
Don't let your differences get the best of us!
You five-pointed stars of the galaxy!
We are all bound together despite your beliefs!"

:MYIOUIEAMICA

DYNAMICA

It is said that the Original Language
is free from the cloak of an alphabet
and that it composes the Book of All Things.

PART THE FIRST. *One and only one.*

The true intimate name of God is and will remain unutterable by the human tongue. That is because it is unpronounceable by an individual.

PART THE SECOND. *Separate and united.*

Alphabet = Alpha-beta, aleph-beth, alif-bayt. These similarities in terms are a reminder that all alphabets/languages are reliant upon one another and that they come from a similar proto-linguistic source, a language closely resembling Akkadian.

PART THE THIRD. *Trinity.*

To pronounce the true intimate name of God successfully will bring about a drastic and immediate change to reality. It is called "The Returning." Humans all over the globe are innately aware of this potential. Every culture has a name for both the individual and collective state of Returning. Some are: Satori, Nirvana, Harmonic Convergence, Dreamtime, Law of One, Eleven-Eleven, and Eden.

PART THE FOURTH. *Four of fours.*

The true intimate name of God must be spoken in *God's* own voice, since it was *God* who created *God*, using *God's* own Word, in *God's* own Language. That voice can only be approximated with an harmonious invocation.

FOUR-ONE.

The true intimate name of God is hidden between the consonants of the alphabet. Not only the English alphabet but within every single human language.

FOUR-TWO.

Between the consonants of the alphabet are the vowels. The true intimate name, the Spirit Name of God exists in consonant "non-space," only the vowels. Vowels are letter-symbols that are practically sung and never struggled over.

FOUR-THREE.

Recitation of the vowels must be performed by all peoples of Earth simultaneously. No one people can do it on their own.

FOUR-FOUR.

God will never hear the name without the inclusion of guttural or glottal vowel sounds that only certain people can pronounce. Every people has a sound they make that is difficult for other people to pronounce. This phenomenon serves a function. This is what unites us.

PART THE FIFTH. *The people.*

In English, the phrase we must invoke is A-E-I-O-U ending with the letter M. M grounds the mouth by closing it down in the form of a flat horizon line, with the lips braced against the teeth, which allows vocal emanations to continue while never interrupting life-giving breath. M completes the wheel of vowels and places it upon the ground, ready for continuing movement.

PART THE SIXTH. *Perhaps confusion.* (fig. 1)

The letters of the alphabet are arranged backward, opposite to their common use. Such is the world of Spirit. Such is the complete world of reflections. Therefore the true order of the cycle of vowels is: (M)-U-O-I-E-A

SO THAT
I + E = dipthong for "I"

AND THAT
A + M = ties the wheel of letters

The phrase, when vocalized, is the English equivalent to the Akkadian mantra and affirmation: "You, oh I am"

PART THE SEVENTH. *Humans in heaven.*

Which leads us to ponder why only "sometimes why" or "sometimes y." Why not "y" every time? *Why only sometimes float freely in the sky unbound?* (Akkadian riddle.) Did not Icarus show us the danger of such excess?

Y is a trickster; a manipulator of truth and interpretation, for Y boldly asks this question: *What confirms that humans are actually allowed to enter heaven and not only permitted to witness it?* Y inspires philosophers to consider alternatives outside their boundaries. The nature of Y also inspired this Lemurian teaser: *When is why, if there is a time?*

PART THE EIGHTH. *Always is not forever.*
The Vowel Wheel, completed, has EIGHT components: if Man is Five, the Devil is Six, and God is Seven, then the genesis power of Everyone would be the number EIGHT.

Tipped on its side, Eight is the symbol of Infinity.

ALSO
Breasts, Glasses, Vessels, Eyes

AND ALSO
the Double Zero.

PART THE NINTH. *In the name.* (figs. 2, 3)
Yah, address for the lord of lords, is to be found in the first square of correlates in the wheel of vowels:

Hayya
Haay
Hayyam
In short, Hayu.

PART THE TENTH. *The tallest building.* (Fig. 4)

Imu'um, breastmilk, a mother's sanctity, her power of forgiving love, is the nature of M. M is the position of the squatting legs of fecundity. M is the action of bearing down upon the earth what was at first only conceptual. From conception to completion, the flow of life energy follows this course: IDEA/concept—WORK/labor, toil—REALITY/physical.

PART THE ELEVENTH. *Side-by-side, never touching.*

"a-e-i-o-u-(y)"

Draws a line in space which meets itself.

"aeiouym"

Is the line, now a spiral, in the natural world.

"myuoiea"

With "m" on the ground is the loop's reflection.

```
"  i
 e  o
 a  u
  m. "
```

Forms a spiral when repeated.

```
"  o
 h  u
 i  o
 a  y
  m "
```

You oh I am is the American English equivalent phrase, which has its own ties to the ancient Akkadian term HU – AY.

The letter square "h-u – a-y" when read counter-clockwise, forms HAYU, which, when transliterated from Akkadian is *hayyu* or "heart" and also "garnet" or "soft red stone of the chest."

The letter square "i-o-m-o" when read counter-clockwise, forms IMOO which, when the final leg of trajectory is brought down to the central "M," indicates the transliteration of Akkadian: *imu'um* or "a mother's love."

The incomplete square is actually a greater symbol: that of a snail, a nautilus, a cocoon, a zygote or gamete.

PART THE TWELFTH. *Mountain scape.*
Numeric equivalents of the American Alphabet; considering the world of completion or the world of reflections which is the domain of inclusion:

A B C D E F G H I J K L M N O P

26 25 24 23 22 21 20 19 18 17 16 15 14 13 12 11

Q R S T U V W X Y Z

10 9 8 7 6 5 4 3 2 1

TUVWXYZ   U = 6   Y = 2
KLMNOPQRS   O = 12
ABCDEFGHIJ   A = 26   E = 22   I = 18

Part the Thirteenth. *The realm.*

Akkadian precepts:

OH I SEE THE ME IN YOU
OH I SEE THE YOU IN ME

Akkadian Word-Concepts:

REFLECTION   SELF REFLECTION
INTERFLECTION   **EPIFLECTION**
PROTOFLEXIVE   PARAFLEXIVE
ENDOFLECTION   EXOFLECTION

Figure 1.

THE VOWEL WHEEL *and corresponding numerals:*

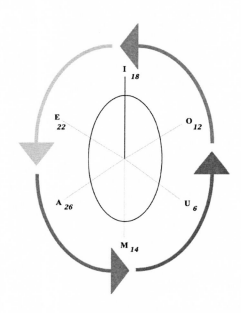

HARMONIC WAVELENGTH JUMPS IN QUANTA
(ENERGY PACKETS) OF SIX OR FOUR:

Akkadian Tenet for the concept DOUBLE = *these are the two of us*
Akkadian Tenet for the concept TRINE = *there is a spirit over us*

MOVEMENT OF THE NUMBERS ON THE VOWEL WHEEL:
U to O: 6 + 6 = 12
O to I: 12 + 6 or 6 + 6 +6 = 18
I to E: 18 + 4 = 22
E to A: 22 + 4 = 26
A to M: 26 - (6 + 6) = 14

Figure 2.

YOU, OH I AM (OH I AM YOU)

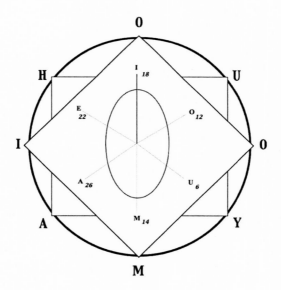

Diagram demonstrating relation to the Vowel Wheel

Figure 3.

HAYU *Trajectory*

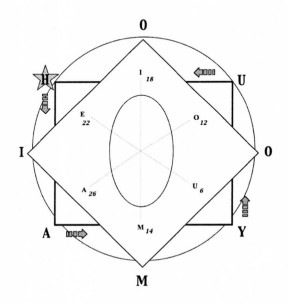

NUMERICAL VALUE:

22 + 26 + 6 + 12 = 66

ALSO WRITTEN AS:

HAYYU

DEFINITION:

"Heart" or "Garnet" also "Soft red stone of the chest"

Figure 4.

IMOOM *Trajectory:*

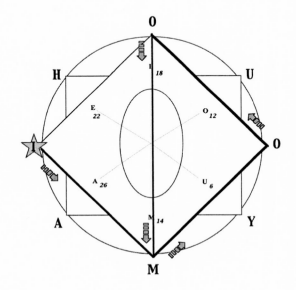

NUMERICAL VALUE:
$(22 - 26) + 14 + (6 - 12) + 18 = 22$

ALSO WRITTEN AS:
IMU'UM

DEFINITION:
"A mother's love" or "selflessness, forgiveness, life-affirming, nurturing"

ACKNOWLEDGEMENTS

This book would not have been possible without the confidence and cooperation of J.K. Fowler and the fierce editing powers of the magical Michaela Mullin at Nomadic Press. I would be shouting my work at the wall, alone, if it were not for the deep, lasting friendships of Paul Corman Roberts, Missy Church, Michael Rothenberg, and John Fair. Thank you to the visual artists who found inspiration in my work, Lena Rushing (lenarushing.com) and Tlisza Jaurique. Thank you also to Sharon Coleman who brought up the massacre of the Communards. Thank you to my early teachers, Burroughs, Green, Dubie, Ai, and Meltzer. Thank you to Codrescu's Exquisite Corpse. Hearty thanks to you, dear reader. In sum, thank you to the legions of operatives too numerous to mention in this brief space, at the edge of the innards, so close to the crust, of this book.

Some of these stories were first published in *Red Fez*, *Full of Crow*, *Big Bridge*, *Rivet*, and *Kleft Jaw*.

About the Author

Youssef Alaoui has spent most of his professional life in library stacks and at the computer referencing worn out facts and citations, researching antiquated wisdom or cutting edge sciences. For a few years, he served as a contracted international investigator. His home cities are Morro Bay, Tempe, Paris, Lille, Seattle, and Oakland.

Youssef is a Moroccan American Latino. His family and heritage are an endless source of inspiration for his varied, dark, spiritual and carnal writings. He earned an MFA in Poetics from New College of California, Mission District, San Francisco. There, he studied classical Arabic poetry, Spanish baroque poetry, and Moroccan contemporary poetry. He is also well versed in 19th century literature of the fantastic.

His writings have appeared in *Exquisite Corpse*, *Big Bridge*, *Cherry Bleeds*, *580 Split*, *Full of Crow*, *Carcinogenic Poetry*, *Dusie Press*, *Tsunami Books*, *Red Fez*, and *Rivet Journal*.

Also by Youssef Alaoui:
The Blue Demon
Death At Sea—Poems